ANN C

Reciprocity

Kerdh Ltd

Copyright 2018 © Kerdh

First Published Great Britain 2020 by Kerdh Ltd

The right of the author, writing under the pseudonym Ann Charles, to be identified as the author of this work has been asserted by them in accordance with the Copyright, Designs and Patents Act 1988.

All rights reserved. No part of this book may be reproduced or transmitted in any form or by any means, electronic or mechanical, including photocopying, recording or by any other information storage and retrieval system without permission in writing from the publishers.

A CIP catalogue record for this book is available from the British Library.

ISBN 978-0-9559650-5-0

Cover Design by Frehja

Printed and Bound in Great Britain by TJ International, Padstow

Acknowledgments-
The publication of this novel has been only made possible
through the guidance and support of:-

CBT Psychological Services Cornwall. St Austell and Newquay
Andrew Henwood Funeral Directors, Newquay
Ralph and Co. Solicitors, Newquay.
Western Permanent Property, Cardiff.
Personal Choice Funerals, St. Austell.
Mr and Mrs P. Jackson.
Elaine Ryder and family.
Mr and Mrs P. Bunt.
Mr and Mrs G. Rickard.
Mr and Mrs G. Hewitt.
Mr and Mrs C. Blount.
Ursula Wesson.
Jocey Hobbs.
Herbie Edge.
Hattie & Hughie Brereton.

And my girls: Frehja, Scarlett, Rosey, Marni, Ysella and Julia.

Reciprocity, from the Latin "moving backwards and forwards."

For Julia x

"The meeting of two personalities is like the contact of two chemical substances: if there is any reaction, both are transformed."
Carl Gustav Jung.

Contents

Prologue- The End	*1*
Chapter One- The Beginning	*18*
Chapter Two- The Return	*32*
Chapter Three- The Preparation	*45*
Chapter Four- The Beginning of the End	*56*
Chapter Five- Now we see in a mirror, darkly	*71*
Chapter Six- The End of the Beginning	*82*
Chapter Seven- Creation	*97*
Chapter Eight- Love	*107*
Chapter Nine- Power	*120*
Chapter Ten- Faith and Resurrection	*140*
Chapter Eleven- Reconciliation	*162*
Epilogue- Reciprocity	*176*

Prologue- The End

It is a sadness in life that, for some, it is in the extra ordinary that life is most clearly visible. We can allow life to get lost in everyday routines. The meaning is still there, always. Life in all its richness is dulled by familiarity, if you let it. Take yourself away, a holiday for example, and let the richness come back. The art of life is to see clearly each and every day. The beauty of each flower. Don't let yourselves be greyed because you see the flower at each opening of the door and yet never see its colours, never appreciate it at all. Rather every day let the freshness of life as experienced in that flower hit your senses directly. Be brought up short by the beauty that is around you, by the joys you share in the life you live. Life is lived when there is no mundanity, no routine. You may well do the same things each and every day through necessity but it doesn't have to feel like routine. For each day is a new day, a fresh day, a forever beginning day.

Isn't it unfortunate that most often, those who express this sentiment do so in lamentation. Like Dives, he wants to warn his friends about the perils of choosing the wrong direction in life, he wants to point them to Lazarus but can't, it's too late. Those who lose a loved one suddenly recognise the missed opportunities to say, "I love you" or recognise those responses which suddenly seem futile and pathetic. Regrets determine the cycle of mainstream Western society; regret, guilt, litigation and recrimination. Regret. To live life. The whole of life without any of these would, in this day and age, be truly remarkable, perhaps unique. There is little point in regretting, unless those regrets spur us to change for the better.

There is an old Irish joke,

"Excuse me, would you be telling me the way to Galway?"

"Galway you say? Well I wouldn't start from here!"

But here is where we are. We may hide ourselves away hermit crab-like in addiction, in work, in fantasy. In the end, should you believe in the end, we are left with only ourselves. What a waste therefore to spend our lives not being ourselves. As on the road to Emmaus our journey may well only be discovering what is already there. In the words of the Irish blessing on death, we are only going home to the home we never left.

Fear of the unknown dominates our lives. The "what ifs" that are either planned out by strategic project management or left to corrode our very existence. Corrosion of self can lead to some very dark places, the dark place of the soul. What has the history of life taught us? That events happen the world over. How do we deal with them? Internalise, reflect. The extent to which we empower them makes the difference.

A criticism of the Christian religion has been in its promise of a heavenly paradise so therefore the status quo of the here and the now should be accepted. "Don't give me pie in the sky". We want our rewards in this life, not in the next.

The boundary between this life and the next, should it exist or should you choose to believe in its existence, is crucial ground for spiritual consideration. When my father died, because of the circumstances, we, that is me, Ysella Mae, and the rest of my grieving family had no moment of closure. Rather the moment was thrust upon us suddenly and there was no secondary moment to collect thoughts and well wishes. It happened, or rather a massive event happened from which came nothing. A vacuum, one moment he was there, the next he was not, not even a body. I took the funeral. I had witnessed him several times during my childhood take funerals. I knew his lightest of touches, his preparedness that looked like he was spontaneous, his back catalogue of poems and phrases stored away 'file like' in his brain. I knew which triggers would provoke which readings. I knew when he was struggling and was unsure if he had got it right, but in the absence of a better alternative would plod on anyway. The unsuspecting family oblivious to his need to get things right at all costs. Particularly to his health. He had been "mostly healthy, never wealthy and seldom wise" he used to lament. Funerals, the taking of them, becomes a myriad of complexities to be woven with just enough loose ends to ensure the continuity of love, not the journey of bereavement, long after the "celebration of life", after the service itself. Unremembered except for a mental picture of mascara panda-ed eyes accompanied with a bag of tissues. Hope, for in the words of Luther King, without hope we lose that courage to be, needs be implicit at times. Explicit hope treads very close to triteness, which in turn closes in on "I'm in the club", which in turn is akin to "I know the answers". In reality we don't.

I used to sit there, when I was older, at the funeral hearing the story of the person, interlaced with the stories of those grieving. In the aspects of those stories there is enough metaphor and allegory to imply the core Christian principles of hope, love and relationship and the doctrines that lay behind them: resurrection, incarnation and the Trinity. Of course almost all didn't grasp the basic theological lessons that have just been delivered using the example of their loved one. Actually good job too.

At my Dad's small memorial I took the essence of what he used to do and put it across in his poems and writings. There was no eulogy as such.

There was disagreement as to who he was. Patient, impatient. Tolerant, intolerant. Happy, sad. Successful; certainly not in his eyes. Abject failure. Which made the timing of his death even more tragic.

Our service, the service that my Dad and I kinda did together, though he did not know it, was not one that would feature on any television programme. No waiting behind to meet and greet. Out in the car and gone. Should the celebrant at a funeral hang around, more often than not they receive the plaudit- nice service. Some even say, I've heard it said to my Dad, 'If you were my Vicar, I'd come to Church.' He turned to a lady once after taking a service in Swansea Crematorium when she had made this ill advised statement and asked where she lived. "Newquay" came the answer back.

"I am your Vicar. So I'll be seeing you at Church then, anytime".

He never did. She never went.

To the seasoned funeral goer, the Priest rarely hits an emotional nerve. My Dad did, but his memorial did not, but then it was raw enough anyway. Once one gentleman came out in tears and said to my Dad, "That was beautiful", to which my Dad replied "Well a beautiful service for Elsie, the least she deserved." The man still distressed exclaimed, "I wouldn't know, I never knew her, I found myself in the wrong chapel and felt too embarrassed to leave. It was a beautiful service though."

Then there is the funeral of a young person. Emotions perhaps more raw that can tear apart the most hardened of professional mourner. Questions of life need to be grappled with before life itself loses meaning. Without knowing it, theodicy, the problem of innocent suffering, permeates such difficult funerals. "Why?" is the question of the hardest of unanswered theological concepts. And don't answer it. Don't try. Merely sit with the question, it is far more rewarding. Rewarding as in, you are not taken off in stupid directions pathetically expecting an answer that makes sense. Instead you sit there, knowing that there is no answer, but the question is no less valid in-spite of this. The question is as old as the book of Job which is interesting if you ever pick it up. Strip away the prose of the prologue and epilogue which, if we didn't know better we could have sworn was written by an American in the deep south in the late 19th century, and you have a poem that answers nothing yet strongly satisfies the spiritual yearnings of the soul. The yearnings that West craves through each different and cyclical fad.

An abiding memory of my Dad was him browsing an orange book by Mark Manson, "The subtle art of not giving a f*ck". The problem was my Dad did; give a f*ck that is. He always cared very intensely what people thought about him, whether he upset anybody. He would do whatever he could to avoid confrontation. In his thoughts he confused avoiding confrontation with keeping the peace. Of course in trying to avoid confrontation he managed to just piss people off especially those closest to him. The Manson was never read. It was the occasion of one of our annual trips to Turkey, a holiday which both my parents yearned for as soon as the previous one had finished. My Dad never stopped working until he was on holiday and then after a week you saw him relaxed, smiling, joking. This was a far cry from the father at work. Vulnerable, sensitive, paranoid believing everybody was out to get him. Indeed some were, but not everybody so every cloud and all that. This was the side of my Dad that my Mum could not understand, abide or tolerate. My Mum, resourceful and ruthless, caring and empowering. My beautiful Mum who only saw the best in Dad. The woman my Dad had worshipped from the moment they had met though he was a slow burner and it took a while before she, losing all patience, lifted her athletic calves and kissed him. They were perfect for each other, complemented each other and though his lack of confidence frustrated her, it was her belief in him that kept him going through his more difficult times. He was always reflecting and self evaluating, partly I think because people tended to be so honest in telling him his weaknesses.

My father told a story of a young woman in hospital he was called upon to visit. Her body was slowly shutting down. She was angry and justifiably so and seeing the cleric of my father walk into her room she flew into a frenzied attack against God, religion and Priests in particular. He agreed with every word, every nuanced attack, deflating slowly her every emotion, then she slept. For eighteen months the girl deteriorated and for the same time he visited her at least weekly. Before she lost the power of speech and had to rely on a signboard to painstakingly spell out words she asked him what a priest did. He joked, "Drink black coffee and put on a face that said 'I'm listening when actually I'm elsewhere.'"

She had seen that face and as her emotion welled inside her she taught him his first definitive lesson in pastoral ministry. A lesson to be in the moment. Not the future, not the past, the present moment. "If you are too tired, too bored or too busy, don't bother." The vehemence with which her impassioned plea was delivered had a profound effect. After that defining moment for him he introduced her to the Beatles back catalogue, "Stop myself getting bored",

"You sod, don't mock the afflicted."

"You mock me all the time and I am a member of an oppressed minority, a clergy person, the most deprived and depraved human beings known to humanity."

He left his prized collection of Beatles vinyl with her. She wasn't going anywhere, he could pick them up when she was bored or whenever……

At the time of her death, her parents who had visited less and less to protect themselves from their own tiredness had decided to place "her" Beatles LP's in the coffin with her. The first time my Father heard of this was during the tribute, delivered by a family friend, at the service. In his relation of the story over several dinner occasions throughout the years he concluded with a question; "What would you do? Run the risk of humiliation and save the treasured collection or see it buried six feet under?"

My Dad's brain never stopped. He was always preparing a speech, an article, a presentation. His mind was always active. Whether driving, working, talking, shopping his mind was always on the next thing. This made him chaotic, leaving the bin bag from the day before somewhere strange having been distracted but forgetting what he was doing so never went back to the bin bag to put it outside. Idiosyncratic tendencies make us individual, make us who we are; that doesn't mean in others they don't frustrate the hell out of us. Dad certainly did that. Too kind, too hard. Too protective, too liberal, too generous, too miserly. He could never quite get the right balance. The years my mother spoke to him about balance, about the grey sides of life, the dangers of everything being black and white. And he believed her. In theory. In practice it wasn't as easy. In life he tended to revert back to his safe position of not upsetting anybody, avoiding confrontation, giving in, not standing his ground. This hadn't always been his way he could be blunt and insensitive and the rebuttals he received led him to clam up so by the time of his middle age and my formative years he was frustratingly more circumspect and continuously needed the support of my mother to simply stand up for himself. He reflected more on sacrifice than strength. He found, of course, in Christ Jesus the ultimate example of this, yet he knew he radically misunderstood this example. He rather used his understanding to fit in with his life events. Christ was his example and Christ relinquished everything for those who hated him. My father then, battered and bruised by life, sacrificed himself to those who hated him.

My Mum stood beside him and gently showed him that strength did not always mean confrontation. She showed him that one could give without being taken advantage of. That silence could both be a strength as well as a weakness. She comforted him, chastised him, got angry with him, but always loved him.

As time went by he slowly became happier. He understood Mum's frustrations, he grew to understand the tempera-mentality of teenagers. He began to understand himself, and through this change which was accompanied by a body that cried out for rest, he began to enjoy each moment for what it was. Gone was the worry over lost minutes of waiting for someone or something. Gradually he learnt to switch off his mind, not plan, not reflect, simply to live. He put on the weight of middle aged contentment, grew a beard tinged with grey on the chin, bristly against my cheek. He found a peace that can only be found within. His body hurt, his mind hurt, but his soul was at peace, a peace the world could only dream of.

Just as he found that equilibrium he….he…..disappeared; no: died. There I said it. He died. Some would say it is ironic, others Murphy's law.

I don't know, whatever the explanation it was dulled by pain.

Turkey, the last day I saw him. We hadn't done anything all day, we just were, my sisters and I. Mum and Dad had kept themselves to themselves, enjoying after more than two decades the honeymoon of married life. It was dark when we found ourselves collected together around the wicker table with its heavy glassed top. My Mum was genius with food. Effortlessly she threw together the most delicious pasta from odds and sods found in the kitchen. Cakes could be rustled up simply in one conversation. Her blond hair delicately falling over her shoulders in the windswept way hairdressers would spend hours coaxing at their models. She had a natural beauty that attracted eyes all around. She attracted attention, none of it wanted. Men leered, propositioned and humiliated themselves. For a woman who laughed off most of life this was the part of life she detested. She didn't understand it for one thing and felt violated. My Dad took this attention very personally. He knew the whole world loved her and she could have anyone in the world. Depending on how he felt it either manifested itself as elation or paranoia, he fought to control the paranoia. Burying those feelings deep inside unhealthily. This then merged with his feelings of never being good enough. Always listening to criticism rather than plaudits. The singer Ed Sheeran once noticed that despite hundreds of thousands of plaudits on his music, the one criticism would ruin his day. My Dad was no Ed Sheeran, but he was the same in this respect. He would break into a slow cold sweat with the slightest of complaints.

My Mum was his backbone and yet despite those negative moments he was hers. You see my Dad was governed by fear of rejection yet he knew by living in this fear he hurt his beloved. He never quite believed that she wanted him. However, as each day passed, their strength of love grew. With a touch of a hand, a look across a crowded room or their warm embrace, cliched yes, true undoubtedly, the precipitation of their lives would lift and in those moments they both grew stronger and he became more and more the man she had loved, knowingly and unknowingly most of her life. In his desire to succeed, my father had tried his hand at many things. Driving himself into an intoxicated frenzy of work and learning. Burying himself, re-inventing himself and pushing all his boundaries of physical exertion, mental agility and spirituality to the extremes. He had become a good runner, once representing his country. A good actor, being offered a place at RADA. He was driven. He had succeeded though it was never enough. My Mum taught him to live in the moment, anxiety free and at these times he wanted to live each moment as if it was his last. I was the apple of his eye, the beautiful little girl, his daughter, the girl who could do no wrong, and yet frequently did.

As a toddler I would tease him. I would scream justifiably for my mother. "Mumma must put me to bed", "Mumma must push my push chair" and yet in pushing him away, in getting my way, I would then reach out and clasp his hand within the safety of my mother's arms. I would let him know, that after-all, he was wanted and I wanted the two of them close. I was instigator and co-conspirator that they may naturally be close to each other. I would snuggle into my Mum, reach out a foot and place into his hand. He was the person I screamed at. He was the person I held. He was the person I rejected. He was the person I searched out. My hero. Always there for me, "Da da?", and he would come. He would be there at my most obnoxious, my most belligerent, taking me in his arms whether I was screaming at him or for him. No matter how big I got. For me he was patient, too patient. If he couldn't cope he would say, "Let's ask mummy what she thinks" and I knew what this meant. His search for moral support, not good cop bad cop, but just checking he'd understood the situation correctly. I knew what this meant and even at aged two I knew which way my mum would go. So at this point I was either compliant or screamed. He adored me, I was the youngest of my sisters and yet the most demanding. Mum had always said that as each girl came along she was surprised that each one was tougher than the last. I was the last of five. Not that I am saying I got away with everything, I most certainly did not. He could shout. A bark that jolted everybody around and then he seethed adrenalin and stress pulsating out of him whether he was quiet or not. I was then calm as I meekly ate my food, or sat down, or stopped throwing whatever I found in my hand.

The house where we holidayed in Turkey was my maternal Grandparents'. My dad loved the countryside, the barrenness of the dry hills towering over the resort-lined coast of the Antalyan countryside. The tomb of St Nicholas was in that part of Turkey. The heat soothed him. The greenery fascinated him. The night landscape intrigued him, the lights of tourist towns dotting across the dark expanse of the horizon. These towns thriving in the summer, a wilderness in the winter. The sounds of the continuous cars did not disturb him, the warmth of the evening nestling and cajoling him into tranquility. He would sit there a glass of red one in hand, reading or talking, listening or writing. The wrinkles from around his eyes would massage themselves away simultaneously as his grey work skin gently bronzed. In Turkey he would not exercise though he always went prepared and invigorated to do so. He lost weight nevertheless. His diet improved, gone were the biscuits consumed by the packetful replaced by fruit and a delicious ice-cream that invariably he just had to share with me. And, because he was wearing swimming trunks, he would hold in his stomach to give himself the stomach to attract his lady-love and to avoid the groans of complaint from my sisters.

My Daddy would do anything for my sisters. He referred to himself as the taxi driver, the bank manager, and yet in reality he was neither. He at the time had no problem with the ferrying and collecting at all hours and yet suddenly when a button was pressed he would change. He would become more of a martyr than Thomas à Becket, lamenting his loss of life in running around down rural Cornish B roads in search of a particular field where one of my sisters would be, bemoaning the loss of his free time or work time. He didn't mind and yet this is what he would throw at us when he was at his most vulnerable. When he was looking for purpose in life. He wanted to please and make happy but when it was never enough he plummeted into the shadows of self pity until my Mum simultaneously lectured him and shouted at us. A kind of bizarre reconciliation where all felt chastised and yet all vindicated in some way. "Enjoy these moments," she would say. "They will soon have flown the nest." He worked so hard to understand the intricacies of adolescent females. Hair through vanity being important. Hair pulled back as a way to avoid irritability. If he complimented he was weird. If he didn't then they missed "You look beautiful". He could never hope to win. He never gave up trying. His strongest lament was that Mum and he had not been together since kindergarten. She was his sole confidante and though, or maybe because of, there was an age gap between my sisters and I, increasingly I became a safe sounding-board. In those years after my sisters had left home, I learnt so much about his work, his philosophical and theological struggles, his life.

His last day with us was uneventful except for the event itself. He simply popped out to get some fruit and water. It was the day before the Turkish community celebrated Eid al-Adha when thousands of animals would be slaughtered and sacrificed. Minutes after he left the house he must have reached the main road. We heard the squeal of brakes, a car or small van hitting something, reversing at speed, doors being slammed shut and the sound of a fast get away. Then we heard the shouts and the screams and we ran. Sixty metres is all it is. The tyre marks on the road still seemed to be smoking. The local traders who knew us came across reporting what they had seen. A far away siren signalled that someone had rung the police but as the fog descended over my eyes I could take nothing in.

We seemed to spend days being interrogated. The police were kind enough to say that they were just trying to piece together a picture, but for westerners it was akin to an interrogation. Describe my Dad? Late 50's over-weight with a beard, but my Dad.

Weeks later it felt like a relief to get back to work. I had done everything I could but to no end. The conclusion; he was dead. He had been in a hit and run, except they had taken the body with them. Dumped over a cliff edge somewhere along the coast.

We had the memorial as a mark of transition. My Mum never gave up hope of finding him. She never will. When it became obvious that staying in Turkey would not achieve anything we left. The night before, my Mum wanted to be left alone. My sisters had already returned to their respective homes and, at a loss for anything to do rather than a concern for her mental well being, I followed Mum down to the harbour at Fethiye.

She cried, tears of bitter pain, of loss, emptiness, numbness, anger, loneliness, confusion, sadness, everything rolled into a seemingly endless roller coaster of emotions that was an intense hit in the moment and yet never ending.

It seems she had come to the shore line, almost by accident, setting off from somewhere to somewhere, somewhere to nowhere, someone and yet here no one. A lost figure in a harbour of busyness, boats touting for the customers of tomorrow. Cafes serenading laughter. She wasn't laughing, she had loved, continued to love and that was the pain. Is it easier never to love and so never to feel the pain of loss? Is it easier to drift in life and then simply to fade away? It would be a waste to drift through; be lonely and yet the pain of love hurt so much. They called it bereavement, but this wasn't bereavement. It wasn't some five stage process of intellectual emotional transference, this was love, a love so deep she was only a part. She had given her soul into the hands of another who had now been lost to her. The slow realisation of the loss of life had embedded away and with it her life.

There were symbols and metaphors, readings and poetry that could be used to explain what was going on but that was all about death. Death was death. Death was pain, but it wasn't this. This was love, the deep soul enriching, experiencing of life that had been ended, but it wasn't the death that hurt, that had to be as the only constant in life, it was the love that hurt. The love that she had control over. For all those years ago when the feelings first stirred within her she could have walked away. She could have hidden them, suppressed and controlled them. She had not, because she had to be true to herself, she had to love as she had been born to love. And that love had been taken, she was now a branch of a tree that was withering from the roots up. One day she would wither too.

She looked at the sea, inviting in its great expanse, her place at the shore insignificant in the great colours and hues of blues and greens overlapping, entwining, topped with a white silver foam of surf ever coming and ever leaving. She noticed a pebble get sucked up the tiny beach and then taken back in the wake of the tide. A pebble that wasn't in control of itself as it got thrown this way and that, becoming smoother over the thousands of years of its creation. It was her. Life was throwing her around. Life had brought her to this shore line at that moment like the pebble and neither of them knew the future.

She looked at it, bent down and picked it up and slipped it into her pocket. It was an unusual pattern, part of a bigger rock, somewhere past, oceans away. But it was part of something bigger, not insignificant and lifeless; part of a bigger story.

She was part of a story, her story with us their children, their friends and memories. A story full of love, that she must retell, for their love, their life needed to be told. The love they shared served as an example. This is what love is. Love hurts. Love doesn't get over it, love continues. Her life would be changed and her love eternal.

The pebble, it would be changed over the years of being knocked back and forth but the pattern lived on in it, in its brother and sister pebbles all hewn from the same rock and perhaps in the cliff face from which it had come. This was her. The pattern of love, a love that had created who she was now standing on the shore line, was not just here but was elsewhere too. Love never changes. This was her hope, not that things would get better, not that somewhere in different ages they would meet again, but that love was stronger than all things, and like the pebble that would survive despite the buffeting of the waters, so would she.

She turned and walked back. Nothing had changed really except now she knew why she hurt, and it wasn't bereavement it was love, and for love she would walk through any pain, it was worth it. She saw me took my hand, smiled and as soft as the wings of a butterfly murmured, "my little shadow." I could not reciprocate, I simply squeezed her hand and we returned in silence. Eventually I murmured. "Why Mum, why the pain? The desolation, the emptiness?"

"Life and love are one for one, made for each other, the other takes it all. The cushioning of heartache, eases the memory. It washes away yesterday and like the ebbing tide the new tomorrow is just a heartbeat away. For just like the river and the sea are one so is life and love. Without the love you share the life with, life is like waiting for the wave, up stream. For life you need to travel to the sea where the risks are greater and yet the achievements unimaginable. You cannot remain in the safety of the river. Join the ocean where experiences are greater though you run the risk of getting swallowed as you search for the wave of life to ride. Taking you beyond what you could never have imagined. The river and the sea are one, remember. Always remember one will take you further. So life and love are one. Each one will inspire you to truly live the other. "

That night when I thought she had long retired to bed, I found her outside on the veranda reading a slip of paper that had been folded and refolded so many times. She didn't lookup, Rioja in hand as she spoke. "Your Dad wrote this. It says it all:-

You have left me but what can I say,
was it just yesterday, feels like forever and a day.
But you are with me as you always were,
In the clear days, and those lost in a blur.

You are the coaster on the breakfast table,
left there forever, for I am yet unable
To put it away hidden in the drawer,
For you always had your coffee there, that I cannot ignore.

You are the coat hanging from the hook.
Yours is the bedside table with its book
still half read, do you now know the end?
I leave it there, just in case, just to pretend.

I know you're gone, it has to be.
It's just in moments each day I will see
You in the small things of everyday.
Then I know you're with me, in every way."

She looked up. "The small mundane things are the extraordinary things. Remember that, Ysella, remember that."

She folded the paper, wiped a tear, beckoned me to turn the light off and we said goodnight to the night.

Chapter One- The Beginning

Demir Baydar lay there. He didn't know what had hit him. Where was he? What had happened? His brain should have been asking thousands of millions of questions all at the same time, something was wrong. He could not quite get a handle on it. His brain was not functioning. He knew, he felt, his body had been through some trauma and yet what was it? Why were there no mental images scrambling through his brain? Where was he? What had happened? Where was he? Oh my God. Who was he?

His brain shut off, his eyes closed and drifted away. No images in his mind just blackness rolling over him like a sea-mist encroaching unwanted over the coast. It was a stillness that western society searches for, spending billions of pounds and dollars per year in self help coaches, mindfulness, yoga retreats, all tried continuously by someone somewhere looking for an enlightenment to heal the fast paced abuses of life. Contemporary spirituality is developing fast paced leaving behind the main stream religions who have embedded themselves firmly in the past.

There will be a new enlightenment when the spirit of the soul communes with the soul of nature. An holistic approach to life, a journey that many had started in the 60's, removing the dichotomy of religion and science. No subservience to an ontological deity beyond, or proclaiming science as the elixir of life, as the great discoveries of Einstein and his nuclear energy and Fleming with penicillin, have the potential to bring about Armageddon. The new enlightenment will be subservient to the here and now. The taking of the moment and assimilating oneself into that moment within the context of that which is around. It isn't really an answer because there shouldn't really be a question. It is just what it is. Now we are at the dawn of this new enlightenment, where the submerging of mind and soul into a clarity of life is real, to understand better the realities that are around. There would be a true self emptying and the readiness to continually start again. Demir's mind was totally emptied. All he had was the blackness, the void.

Demir's father looked over him. Years before his own training in the foothills of Afghanistan taught him, that for the body and mind in front of him, this was a blank slate. A person to be created and therefore a man to bring about change. Swift, radical, decisive and above all, for the better. But that was for the future. Now was for healing and rehabilitation and looking down at the battered body before him, he knew it was a long journey ahead of him, ahead of them. He was Ahamd Baydar and he sat in the Turkish Village of Kabak. Small enough that strangers stood out, rural enough that no-one really cared. The strains of everyday life draining all energy to worry about others. The bed with its IV drips pumping antibiotics, glucose and painkillers into the limp arm that lay unconscious. It was a forced coma. The shock of the accident damaging the mind, the internal organs, the bones. Recovery was going to be all consuming. He had been rushed to the makeshift room in this tiny village. No one knew where he was, who he was. His son was now safe. If his life had any meaning where was it pointing to at this moment?

Demir was to open his eyes a couple of days later when gently the coma inducing drugs had been withdrawn. He went to speak but could not. The old man gently encouraged him to drink from a flask of water, tepid, it tasted disgusting. The old man nodded enthusiastically.

Somewhere overhead in the background were voices. He understood bits but everything was a blur. He closed his eyes, his head sunk deeper into the pillow and his mind voided again.

He didn't know how long he had slept for but when he awoke, the old man wasn't there but the voices were. He looked up and noticed the speaker overhead. The voices were imperceptible. Why had the speaker been placed there? Was it to keep his mind alive? He went to move out of the bed and slid off into a pile of sheets and tubes. The drips and monitors thrown into mess around him. He tore at the drips that had not removed themselves and sat there perspiring heavily.

The old man walked in, nodded and sat down.

They simply sat motionless staring at one another.

The silence was ok. It was a mutual recognition that some things are best unsaid. It wasn't power, it wasn't subjugation, it was a simple acknowledgment that sometimes words are meaningless. The old man stretched out his hand, grasped the younger man's hand and gently encouraged him back onto the bed. Demir eventually spoke a halting Turkish as if he had just left a radio play.

"So you are here then."

The old man looked quizzically at his son and replied.

"My son, my son"

No embrace only the smallest hint of sentimentality.

"Where am I?"

"You are safe now. You are Demir- of Iron, you will last a long time, your name foretells it."

That was enough for now, he closed his eyes once more and drifted as the voices overhead continued. Days merged and during the brief moments of waking he ate, till exhausted he fell back to sleep again.

Then, days later, he didn't know how many days he was woken by his sense of smell. An aromatic moussaka had been brought into the room, been placed on a side table with a fork and left. He leant across, the tubes and wires had been removed from the room completely, only the bloodstained bandages remained as evidence of their use. The food was devoured, he felt he hadn't tasted anything quite like that.

He waited for twenty minutes to let the food settle on his stomach. Indigestion was quite painful, the stomach still acclimatising. He then begun to move. He hurt. He assessed his body, two broken legs in plaster. Both arms aching. Broken ribs he thought. He thought a catheter had been removed. This was a good sign. He checked his pulse rate 110. High but probably accurate. The flesh on his stomach was sore. He studied it.

"Infected". His father walked into the room. "We are treating it with antibiotics."

"How?"

"The blast."

It was a reply that closed the conversation and invited no further questions. But what blast?

The following morning he felt decidedly stronger so when his father walked into the room he was already propped up.

"You're better!" A statement, not a question, and as the door closed he realised that the sun was shining. That door was an outside door! This room was the building itself. He looked around, it was basic and functional and yet new. The floor was tiled, the walls painted. His metal bedstead and mattress were new and everything was spotless.

"Where am I?"

"You are home. I've nursed you myself. Not a bad job if I say so myself." They both smiled.

Demir was searching for the words to formulate a conversation. His vocabulary was found wanting. He recognised that his pronunciation was no better. It was as if he was relearning his mother tongue.

"Can I help?"

Was his father sensing his thoughts? He closed his eyes, weariness once more got the better of him. The drugs that had been administered before he had awoke now took effect. They say sleep is the best medicine, he didn't know, he didn't actually care, not really. He just let it take over him letting go of consciousness and accepting the warm embrace of sleep once more.

Kabak is a hamlet thirty minutes outside of the tourist beach resort of Oludeniz. Climbing the narrow winding roads with its hair-pin bends Kabak is the merging point of traditional rural Turkey and tourism. Now it is dominated by differing tourist accommodation. Signs pepper the drive up the hills, "Treetop houses", "Mamma's Pansson". It was to the Olive Garden that Demir had been brought. Ahmad had been drawn to the secluded vantage point above the bay. The Olive Garden had small separate chalets, each with electricity, toilet, shower and air conditioning. The month before, as if he had had a premonition, he bought the Olive Garden. It was just before the close of the season and he had let the managers continue until the season's end. He had then told them to take a three month holiday, which he paid for, cash, which left him now in silent solitude with Demir. The season had been poor and the staff were delighted that they had a job to return to at all. No one would have been surprised if he had laid them off. He didn't. So they left elated rather than filled with questions. The war in neighbouring Syria, the muted and ever present threat of IS or any of its individual lunatic fringe, the unstable political climate in Ankara meant the Daily Mail reading British package holiday tourist looking for an English fry up, had stayed away. No one knew the Olive Garden had a new owner excepting the managers. No one knew of the extent of his wealth. Like his Soviet enemies in the Afghan foothills he had discovered similarly to countless others through the centuries before him, war meant money. Baydar had the backing of the west against the Russian invader. He had no friends, he was unique and he had prepared for this moment, a moment when he could give this middle aged man, his son, a new chance of life.

War, as is well documented, changes the lives of all the protagonists. Those who stand back and direct the pawns are no nearer the frontline than the politicians back home. They are left with guilt and recrimination when the numbers become names and names become personalities and the personalities people, people with families, parents, children. Those on the frontline see life taken and abused on both sides; smell the sulphur and the poison; step in the blood and excrement; see the body parts mutilated beyond recognition, their insides turned out. The brain, unwilling and unable to comprehend these atrocities, survived. As a commander in the Mujahideen, Baydar tasted both the smell of sulphur and the self-recrimination of being a leader. He knew his foot soldiers as keenly as he knew his senior colleagues. The caves they shared together where hunger and tiredness were bed-fellows and, mixed with a toxic blend of hatred and religion, created a cocktail of fundamentalism that knew no boundaries.

Ahmad converted to humanism. Radical humanism. Religion was answerable for so much in the world. Not that he went down the easy well trodden path of blaming religion for all wars, he nevertheless recognised that the religious leaders of all times turned a blind eye to war, secretly craving a greater monopoly for themselves. Profiteering in war is not just down to money. Humiliation of the enemy, especially their ideology and culture, profits the religious authorities far more than money. Ahmad's conversion was as radical and fundamental as any member of the Taliban youngsters who had been growing in strength within the Mujahideen. He had respected them. Their lack of superficial hypocrisy in rejecting American dollars, the very dollars he had accepted that had got him out, he found appealing. To fight for an ideal was laudable but he knew when ideals weren't achievable then more mundane influences maintained the cause. The opiate trade was the clearest reason why all the superpowers were so interested in this mountainous backwater of a country. The war had made him tough, resolute and tired. Very tired. The war needed to be fought differently. The war of attrition on both sides only caused ever increasing numbers of casualties. The conflict at the end of the twentieth century was being fought in the same way as it had been by the British at the century's beginning. War needs to be true war, all people on the frontline fighting for their homes, their livelihoods, their very existence. Not based on flawed ideologies and fairy tales. War is the elixir to the world's ills, its suicide mission in destroying the environment, God's creation. Humanity's hell bent policy of destroying itself by destroying each other over words. The civilised world, which is an oxymoron in itself, needs for its own sake to destroy itself and there needs to be a catalyst. Ahmad saw himself as the catalyst, although history would probably not shine favourably on him if he failed. He would be Dr. Frankenstein and his son lay in front of him, stitches criss crossing his body, hiding the metal pins that held it together. He looked at the world and got depressed. It needed to re-invent itself, to press the reset button. A true resurrection of the phoenix from the ashes and he would create the ashes. He would be Abraham, sacrificing his new born in the cause of a better world, but unlike Abraham, he would go through with it.

As soon as Demir was strong enough Ahmad provoked a conversation.

"You have read and read and you know so much in theory. Life though is not about theory. It is about experience and experience changes the theory. Scientists are those of us who question why, how, what, when, where. And they are never satisfied with the answers which is why we keep finding out new and wonderful things, forever changing our perceptions of the reality we take for granted. Life is predominated by making decisions. When our ability to make a decision is impaired we lose our humanity, reacting and frequently lashing out. Decisions and control are close bed-fellows. Decisions happen every millisecond. Decisions dominate our lives yet so many of our decisions are actually a fait accompli for cultural norms and experiences influence us so much that anyone with half a brain can second guess another action. The motives behind our decisions are the subjects of our reflection. Pure, honest, spiritual reflection of caring for others will evidence that sometimes we do things out of a sense of duty. Across all societies from the US through Europe to Japan there are workaholics. Take this example,...."

He placed down an article from Japan. The "karoshi deaths". Mira Sado's death was attributed to "karoshi", death by overwork. Miss Sado had worked 159 hours of overtime in a month and had died because of it. In one year alone, 107 deaths had been attributed to "karoshi". Personal motivation to drive oneself into the ground, and for what? The protestant work ethic was not just protestant.

"People across all sectors of every society have a lack of self confidence or even self loathing which for some is exacerbated by outside influences causing unhappiness or lifelessness. Finding life in all things is in honour of the creative God, not just that which makes us feel better. That is why religions seem to be getting everything wrong. They want to somehow gain converts by giving them a selfish reason to convert. Being a radical humanist is the impression that is needed to be given for the world to take notice. A mere hint of God and no-one will take you seriously, they will put you in a box, put you in a corner and get you out each time they need a soundbite that fits in with the popular movement of the moment. And people willingly play the game. Look at social media. Life is measured now in terms of likes and popularity is a double edged sword. Mistakes in this day and age are costly because they are too public. Michael Gove, a British government minister gets slated for an inappropriate joke on national radio. The lunacy is that everybody laughs inwardly but pillory outwardly to further their own careers or position or social standing. Comedy is a curtain behind which sadness ferments. Bill Hicks, an American comedian, made universal home truths acceptable by doing so with joy. Yet personally he struggled, he fought. Comedy from a point of happiness, not self loathing and fear, is desirable. Yet it is hard to find in western society. Hope with joy changes lives even at the death bed."

He paused, he was rambling as he always did when talking about that which was so important to him. He could never quite get everything into a suitable soundbite. He was too old for this world of soundbites. He no longer fitted in. Thinking and philosophy seems to have been lost to the world, when everything that is inside can be summarised by a few pithy words, meaningless yet liked on Facebook by 56 million faceless "friends".

"Understanding and knowing those around you is essential and yet at the same time always hit and miss. There are so many variables when it comes to personality, so many exceptions, in one's own life, to the rule. A life of decisions and risks, how do we react when the risk pays off, how do we react when it doesn't? Continuously we are adapting and changing. Sometimes a situation, very often clouded in love, means that we will no longer see in a mirror, dimly, but we shall see face to face. This makes for extreme vulnerability. Vulnerability can bring the best out of someone close, but it can turn into a rabid dog very quickly. Just being there, wherever there is, is enough. That is being, so powerful. And on the other side is the doing. So damaging. In the West they call it the protestant work ethic. If you just be, you are lazy. If you do, you are a workaholic. You can't win. Sportspeople, politicians, actors they put on pedestals and then spend the rest of their time trying to knock them off. Jesus of Nazareth couldn't win either; in Luke we find:- "For John the Baptist has come eating no bread and drinking no wine; and you say, 'He has a demon.' The Son of Man has come eating and drinking; and you say, 'Behold, a glutton and a drunkard, a friend of tax collectors and sinners!' If you want to bring comfort you also need to bring prophetic words to all, making known through the sacrament of life the eternal word- and that word is love. Those that truly live are responding to love. Your mother and I went to an English wedding once and it struck me that they use a line from St John's Gospel to begin the service but it is lost in the mayhem of the arrival of the bride: God is love, and those who live in love, live in God and God lives in them. So much beauty and meaning in that one line and like so much beauty in the world it is lost through familiarity. The world is losing touch with the beauty around us. Savour it, treasure it , love it. Life is transitory. You have taken a step back, so now stop and see the world in all its beauty. It could be lost unto itself and yet you have the key.

None of us can control much really. We can do our utmost to put ourselves in a position where risk is minimised. Yet the most important times in our lives tend to be those times where risks are at their greatest. A project manager's nightmare. The "in-the-moment" risks which no amount of planning can prepare for. Yes be prepared, I will prepare you, but above all live in the moment where the dark cloud of unknowing means you simply have no idea how you got there and what happens next."

Demir laughed. "But that is me, where I am right now......" He faded off recognising of course that his father was meaning exactly that. Now was the moment to take the opportunity to reassess life because life had reassessed him.

Once he was able to walk he quickly began to run each morning taking in every feature of the countryside. Living the moment. He found running natural, with an easy gait that ate up the kilometres, and soon he was fitter than he had even been. There is a great spirituality in running. The freedom from life and the oneness with nature. In his running he thought of everything he had read in the books his father provided on a Kindle. He devoured the knowledge, the thirst for it never wilting. The two of them discussed, debated and analysed and disagreed. The questions of identity were purged in a work ethic that rivalled the Japanese. The moments when he stopped therefore were stark and harsh and the questions welled up within, almost tormenting and certainly disorientating any sense of equilibrium. All functionality was lost in these moments and he simply gave in to the stirrings of memories and the futility of suppression. Prepared for such an "attack" on one such occasion he sat down on the shore and wrote.

"See it whilst standing; acknowledging, submerging, let go of all that is within. Watching the torrents become ever smoother. Slowly vanishing out of sight, the ebb and flow of the tide. See within whilst sitting; Wrestling, arguing with the true self, letting the self win. Against all the buffeting of the world. Slowly becoming stronger and letting it go like flowing water. See without whilst praying; Silencing the still small voice of anger, hurt, letting it go.

Into a flood of past and future worries. Letting yourself be purified and washed with flowing water."

Praying? What was this urge to immerse oneself into a bigger reality. What was this inbuilt inclination? Was it nature, certainly not nurture. Did this account for the innateness of religion? At the same time there was something else also lurking within. He wasn't angry, simply lost. Solid memories weren't returning, merely artificial feelings unrooted and sporadic. He undertook therefore to adopt this identity which felt uncomfortable, like wearing someone else's suit that was slightly too small.

Day after day he read, learnt languages; English, French and Russian. He exercised, he rested. By the start of the following tourist season the scars had healed except the one across the abdomen. It itched, it pained him, it oozed pus. The painkillers and anti-inflammatories grew stronger. Omeprazole was also taken to protect the stomach. The conflict of feelings across the skin were unbearable. His father came in one day with a steroidal cream.

"Use it sparingly. One finger tip for the whole area." Within three days he felt better, although the discomfort was still there, it was bearable. The daily sweat had for months aggravated the abdomen so why had it taken so long for his dad to find a treatment? He didn't ask. Like so many questions he didn't ask. He never asked about his mother, his family.

As his father got to the door of the room, he turned. "Damir, I have tried to teach you the major languages of the world. Now we need to put you to the test. You will work as a waiter here in the Olive Garden serving the tourists. Speak their language wherever you can. Charm them. It would be good to make this place a success, it would be good for you."

That night, as he looked to the stars and found himself part of a bigger world with bigger ideas yet shackled to this world unable to know how to get out because he had no understanding where the metaphorical ground was so he could plant his feet firmly and stably. He prayed.

The words barely audible even to himself were spoken not thought.

"O Lord, my heart trusts you but I do not trust myself. My mind searches for you but easily it's lost. My soul yearns for you but does not know where to start. I will dedicate my life to you if I understood dedication. I ask for your help because I am scared and feel I have the wrong road from which there is no turning back. So I pass this over to you. For into your hands, O Lord, I commend my Spirit."

Chapter Two- The Return

At 5.30am the alarm tone sounded, as it had done since her college days, on Filippa's phone signifying the start of another long work day. She reached for it to see who was doing what, where, and with whom on the varieties of social media. It gave her a head start on gossip. Gossip, the currency of the fashion industry. As a young designer she had taken that world by storm by winning at 19 the prestigious Council of Fashion Designers of America, and the first Brit at that. She transcended all worlds, crossing effortlessly between all boundaries not by some driven desire for power but rather simply and humbly loving what she did. She had been brought up in rural Britain but that was irrelevant now. Her name was Filippa. Spelt the Nordic way, it was her fashion label, her identity, her life.

She reached for clothes, picked out the night before, for "you have to look your best darling" which was not a statement of intent rather a sanguine statement regarding the world she now enjoyed and possessed. She had never taken herself too seriously. She did though take her work seriously, tirelessly ensuring every stitch was perfect, always demanding the best from herself and her staff.

She simultaneously dressed, keyed her phone and flicked her hair away irritatingly, a habit she had nurtured at school which gave a warning sign to those who were about to approach when she simply wasn't in the mood. Breakfast, a staple of her day, fruit and yogurt with a ladle full of honey consumed, and never once is there a pause as her fingers swiftly and expertly guide their way across the screen keys of the latest iPhone. This was the last day of work before a trip to Turkey;

Ovacik between Oludeniz and Fethiye. She deserved this holiday. It would be nice to catch up with two of her sisters, to relax, to get away, to be.

West across the M4 her sister Sapphire, one of a twin with Ruby, both girls names reflecting their personalities, colourful and vibrant and yet sensitive and vulnerable. Sapphire ran her father's business whilst he took early retirement and drank Sangria in Spain. She had an aptitude for it, her vivacious personality that wrapped everybody, men and women, round her little finger. She had the ability, it was said, to look you straight in the eye, tell a bare faced lie and yet despite all logic you would believe her. Not that she was dishonest, her company WPPC had been investigated many times by the HMRC and every time was found to give exemplary record keeping. No cash in hand, everything down to the last penny was accounted for on her watch and she never spent a penny more than she had to. The business was streamlined, it could metaphorically fly into space it was so efficient. She was ruthless; turning the knife in on a deal whilst smiling the protagonists into thinking that they were getting just what they needed. She was beautiful like her sisters. Flying to Turkey meant that a day was needed to pack. She knew that basically all she would wear would be a bikini, a pair of shorts and flip flops but still, she smiled to herself, a girl can never be too prepared. The smile was short lived, it was first thing in the morning. No-one smiled first thing in the morning. What was there to smile about? She had been told she was not a morning person. "Who is?" she had responded. "Compared to you, everybody." She had snorted at this, turned on her heels and ended the brief conversation. Things, people, whatever just annoyed her, more in the morning than any other time. There was nothing for breakfast, there was too much choice for breakfast. The kitchen was untidy, the kitchen was too tidy so she couldn't find anything. She got annoyed and first thing in the morning was as explosive as dynamite.

Ruby, identical twin physically, could not be more different. An international award sat upon her shelf in her bedroom for her work in saving endangered species. Fiction has long included accounts of people who could talk to animals. From Kipling to the Thornberrys, talking to animals remained the privilege of the imagination. Not so with Ruby. Animals sought her out, came to her to be loved by her. Ruby knew no different in her life. From a tiny age and her cats and fish, animals responded to the gravitational aura that surrounded her. She didn't need fiction, she lived it. She didn't need accolades either. All she needed was animals, their safety and their strength and her strength in their weakness. But the award was hers. It was deserved. She had put herself in danger unwittingly so many times in the cause of saving every living creature and had become quite a legend. Like both her sisters, she never backed down. She was right, always had been, always was, always will be.

The three girls arrived unnoticed at Gatwick at different times from the A303, the M4 and the M3. Unnoticed to all but passport control. The three Greene girls were together for the first time in a year. Each stunningly beautiful. Together as they passed through customs slowly and gradually every head turned. Imagine if you will, the very first Virgin Atlantic television advert and then make it real. There you had it. Faces that the unsuspecting tourist recognised but not quite sure where from. Men looked longingly, their wives jealously bringing them back to reality by jabbing their husbands in the ribs.

Turkey, the land of boundaries epitomised by its minarets and the MacDonalds. The land where Europe meets Asia. Friend of the West and neighbour to the East. Liminality, on the threshold with a rich past and an uncertain future. The brown mountains towering above the picturesque national park at Oludeniz with its crystal turquoise sea. A tourist town in the south where the optician's major trade is with the English tourist and the restaurants' menus are littered with minor spelling mistakes in English. Up the hill is Ovacik, a village aspiring to be a town, midway between the tourist centre and Fethiye. A stone's throw from the region's own Blackpool minus the tower but plus everything else; Hisaronu. The area encircled by mountains and water, traversed by a highway of criss-crossing Dolmus hurtling towards paradise or oblivion. The loud Mosque with its neon red, green and white advertising, displaying meaningful verses from the Koran, whilst 1000 miles away IS disintegrates as a multi-nation state without borders or sense of identification with international law. Here the tomatoes and figs and a multitude of vegetables grow abundantly in an earth that sees bucketloads of rain at intermittent times. During the summer, gardens for the English tourists are watered daily by the locals earning just enough to pay the bills. Do not leave your loose change by the pool, it won't be there in the morning and language can be such a barrier to communication when it wants to be.

The rich from Istanbul also holiday there, bringing their whole family of grandchildren still in their twenties supervised by the patriarch and matriarch who dress as if they are going to water the gardens of their English neighbours who could never hope to have the kind of money these rich cosmopolitan peasant-dressed entrepreneurs have made.

These holiday villas share pools. Families share with couples, English and Turks. You will stereotypically find an overweight retired couple coming out at 11 to soak up the rays for their leathery skin and on each entry to the pool causing a veritable Tsunami to the other side.

Life is about holding the balance between two opposite forces. Oxymorons, contradictions, exceptions to the rule permeate our very existence. Modern Western lifestyle seems to have, at its nirvana, a paradise where these tensions disappear. Not through any spiritual harmony of understanding or enlightenment, rather through a power-drive money-orientated quest to obliterate that which is disagreeable. In politics it is thinly veiled as strong government. There is nothing worse than a democratically elected strong government with the mandate to do what it likes. For soon enough comes the excesses and the reactions pulling the political climate to the other side of the pendulum. Life is therefore a constant, sometimes soporific journey of crossroads and u-turns. Many of which are navigated time after time from all directions. The only constant being the monotonous change. In the East it is seen as cyclical, in the West as linear as the East Coast railway line cutting unceremoniously yet purposefully across England.

The truth is of course probably neither. Life is life. Explanations are simply forms of words to enable some comprehension to those who question that they may merely carry on. Questions veil a greater part of life. In answering these questions, or at least in trying to answer them, a large part of life is consumed! Wasted? Paradoxically though to save wasting our lives asking questions, we need to ask THE question; what is the purpose of life? We all have asked this question and perhaps found an answer that enables us to contrive our meanderings through the field of life. Liminality and Turkey seem synonymous. A good place to ask

THE question, to contemplate THE future, but don't lose sight of the present. Life is what happens whilst you are trying to control it.

The girls had holidayed in Turkey for years. It often marked the period of transition in the summer. GCSE results were emailed across from friends during the summer family vacation. Then A levels, and degrees. Preparations for the new chapter always ensued. Bargain hunting and bartering at the shops, bazaars and markets. It marked some of the happiest times and some of the saddest. Illness intermingled with laughter. Recreation mingled with the constant buzz of emails demanding ever more and more. Each time, as they grew up they promised themselves, this year would be relaxation and the phones turned off. But fashion houses, tenants and animals did not go on holiday, problems need to be solved 24/7. In between times though, sun, alcohol and sleep.

This year was different. All three girls had thrown themselves into their jobs in the preceding year, never looking up to catch breath. Quality was matched with quantity and they were now tired. Not just physically but mentally and if they cared to admit it emotionally and perhaps spiritually. But they didn't talk about such things. Theirs was the life that was intimately private. People thought they knew them, but they only revealed what they wanted. The whole package was deeper and mostly unsaid even unto themselves. This year was the year of the boundary, marking a definitive movement away from the past. This year it was only the three of them. This was the first and most significant change. No watchful eye of parents waiting up until they'd partied themselves out. This was the year of transition.

As they entered the villa at two in the afternoon strangely uncomfortable for a place they knew well, Filippa cast a glance to the other two. It said, loud and clear as if had it come from the speakers that lined the thoroughfare through Ovacik- not a word. The twins looked down. They had spent the year quite happy not to talk about the previous year, they knew Filippa had taken it the hardest of the three of them. They knew that if they were to keep her on this vacation then no reference to the betrayal, the absence and the total irrationality of the incident, that time could never be mentioned.

They dropped their bags and went straight to Kabak. The Olive Garden. The restaurant and pool were open and they could be pampered with sun and cocktails all afternoon. The waiter continuously refilled their drinks. His English was perfect. Filippa at one moment started to speak in French, it was second nature to her and he responded in equally as good French. She was impressed. She ordered their food in English and he replied in a strange language. She looked puzzled.

Sapphire interceded, "Russian."

Raised eyebrows all round. "I dated a Russian footballer for a few months. How else do you think I got my diamond necklace?" They all laughed, lightening the mood. When they ate, they ate in silence. Some things remain unsaid.

The first morning began as most holidays throughout the world do. They slept in. A long hard fought night had finally been tamed and each of them had slept. They awoke. Bedraggled they meandered down the marble staircase to the kitchen area, barely greeting an audible grunt as if they had returned to their teenage years once more. Tea, coffee and a fruit concoction were consumed and the day planned. Like most non-package holidays, food shopping was high on the agenda. It was Tuesday; Fethiye market day with its tables and tables of tomatoes, figs, honey and Turkish delight. Sauna like intensity of heat, a cacophony of sound that to the detached observer almost had a melody to it. A resonance to the past, echoing markets of two thousand years ago.

Once inside you cannot remain detached. You are called, cajoled, persuaded and escorted to visit stalls of belts and handbags, "genuine fake Nike shoes". From the oldest man turning his wood majestically into bowls, to the little girl selling braids and anklets, everybody had a place and the Westerners' place was to hand over the well bartered money and feel relieved to escape the intense humidity and heat that made decision making not so much based on rational thought but more reactive emotion.

For a while the girls lost themselves, each carrying bags and bags of provisions. They ate Turkish food; they didn't need the "Pork Shop" in Hisaronu that sold all kinds of expensive Western products like "Lea & Perrins". Once the market experience was over, their senses satisfied and intoxicated with spices and aromas only dreamt of in even the most cosmopolitan parts of Camden or Notting Hill, then the grim reality of the vacuum of this time hit.

A few years previously, as they began to hit the pinnacle of their careers, they had flirted together with the high life and the Cardiff and London high society. Their pictures, for a brief period only, could be seen in the party snaps of the rich and famous. For a moment they were akin to the Hiltons, but with less money and more brains. They had tasted that life but it wasn't for them. So they quickly disappeared and resumed normal life away from the paparazzi and closer to their long-term friends who knew them before the success. The kind of friends everybody should have, the friends who keep you grounded, keep you true and honest. In truth, friends.

At this moment as they sat on the Dolmus the space was deafening and they needed something. Sapphire was essentially the party goer, though she had learnt the tools of the trade from her older sister. Ruby was more reserved but, as had been the case in their early childhood, always fitted in. Not that she didn't have her own mind. She most definitely did. Passionate, animals were not only a vocation they were her sanctuary. In her world she was accepted and she was happy with that for she never really felt accepting of the world, of a society, that could treat animals so abhorrently.

"I know, paragliding!" The first sentence of the whole journey and yet it began where it needed to, at the end where their thoughts were.

"No."

"Oh go on."

"No."

"Well, I am." Defiance was an attribute Sapphire had perfected. Not necessarily because she knew something was right, more that she felt something was right and therefore that was good enough.

"Yep, guess I will." said Filippa, more out of a sense of loss for an alternative than anything else.

"Great. So either I wait for you or I jump off a cliff again." Ruby had paraglided once and sworn it was an experience that she needn't do again. The reason why birds flew, they had wings.

"Go on, you know you want to." Sapphire teased, using her charm that even though Ruby was very aware of its use as a tactical weapon, she succumbed.

They stepped off the Dolmus outside of the Teras pub, walked across the road and up the small hill to the villa. They put the food away and purposefully walked into the direction of Hisaronu.

"H" tours with its luminous yellow sign advertising every kind of activity from mud baths to jet skiing is down on the right before the main thrust of Hisaranou. They are a travel agent, signposting and making a cut. A hard graft of a living especially when the seasoned tourist is ready and willing to walk away unless the bartering has been positive in their favour. The Greene girls were seasoned tourists.

"That was a good deal in the end", smirked Sapphire after they had walked away.

"He was just happy to see us go" bounced Filippa.

"Have we time for lunch?", Ruby was bending down giving attention to an owned dog languishing in the shade of a shop doorway.

So lunch in Oludeniz it was. The Buzz Bar, famed for its cocktails but today just for its club sandwiches. The cocktails would wait until the evening, until after the descent off the mountain.

"Priamson" was the paragliding firm of choice used by Hannibal. And it was Priam's men and mini-bus that traversed the looping road up to the launch site, high above the peninsula.

The cloud was coming in and Sapphire, ever mindful for her twin sister, tried to ensure that Ruby would jump second. The unsaid agenda throughout their lives between Filippa and Sapphire had been to protect Ruby. That didn't meant that Ruby didn't frustrate, annoy and anger them, but Ruby was more vulnerable, more naive and Sapphire being the twin had always understood that. Filippa hadn't quite got the hang of it but understood Ruby's vulnerability.

The pilot behind Filippa started to run toward the cliff edge. Filippa's adrenaline pumping let out a scream and she looked at Sapphire. Sapphire was already on her way, the two instructors were parallel as they stepped off into oblivion. The clouds below them were closing in on the opportunity to jump. Filippa felt the moisture against her face. Where's Ruby? Sapphire craned her neck to get a glimpse of her sister, the video cam on her helmet videoing the fabric of the red and white parachute.

Freedom is very precious. Western Society seems to lament that which it hasn't, the more it actually has. Freedom to talk, walk where you want to. Freedom to defy gravity in many different ways. Freedom of choice. Money can create further choices, further opportunities but freedom is one of the key attributes of happiness. The feeling of being free, having just jumped off a cliff is dependent on your ability to determine how you can control where you go while you float. If you have no chute, then there is no freedom as gravity simply controls your body. If you are fortunate to have a chute but are strapped to an instructor who controls your ultimate destination then you lose the existential feeling of simply floating in the air. Filippa and Sapphire would both have liked to jump solo to experience the elation and satisfaction of being in control of their own freedom. For the time being though they were strapped, each to a Turkish instructor who seemed monosyllabic and oblivious to their obvious concern for the third sister. The two girls were too far away to establish any meaningful communication so as they continuously scanned the sky above them, which was darkening at each moment, their fears increased.

"Where is she, where is our sister?" The unison of voices from the two Greene girls who had landed was shrill.

"Don't worry, she come by bus," Priam responded, his expansive hands locked in front of him.

"You said that an hour ago," Filippa threw back her hair taking it away from her face.

"They have many people to transfer; she safe, she safe." His phone blinked a text message. Filippa snapped it up. The blood drained from her face. A few short words that could mean anything except it was sinister. A blunt, "*Ona sahip.*" Not, "*Soon be with you*", "*Ona sahip.*"

"What does it mean?" Sapphire was panicked by her sister's reaction.

"We have her."

"Well of course they have her." The younger sibling was not comprehending the enormity of the situation.

"Don't be afraid, some friends just want to teach your little sister a few manners. She and her animal-loving friends have cost my clients a lot of money with their shenanigans." Priam said with obvious relish. He was going to make a lot of money over this. Three high profile international girls who had holidayed in Ovacik since their primary years, everybody knew the Greene girls. He knew they were in the country by the time they had opened the front door to their Grandparents' Turkish residence. Filippa was growling at him.

"I'm Greek, studied Philosophy at Manchester Polytechnic as it was then, but this place, easy life, easy money."

"Give our sister back!" The shrill unison was back.

"Go to your place and wait. No harm. Just keeping her out of the way for a few days."

At a loss, the girls faces cast down, left the office.

When they were out of ear shot Sapphire hissed, "Well do something, ring the police." There was no response. "Filippa". Still no response.

"Well, I will."

"Pointless" was the muted response. "Let's call the Embassy."

♦

"Ysella!" It was a normal day until a phone call came through to the boss and I had happened to be in his line of vision. So two hours later I was on a plane out of Gatwick to find out about the disappearance of one Miss Ruby Greene. Calls from High Places. It was looking like a bit of a public relations disaster for the Turkish authorities. High profile animal rights campaigner taken hostage but later found in a police cell. My job was to go there and look at the evidence against her and assist the authorities. She was well known for what she believed in, she got angry but never broke the law. But this was Turkey. The Rule of Law was, shall we say, more arbitrary than in England. Though at times I do wonder about our country. Oludeniz has a police station which is where I was driven to, only to find she had been shipped to Ankara just an hour before.

"For her safety," the man in uniform had said.

"Bollocks." My non-verbal response must have been obvious. He didn't care. I was a woman. I was English. I had no jurisdiction. I rang my Boss. I was told to come home. I tried to argue. He knew I would take any opportunity to stay. To find my Dad, maybe. It was a year. I just wanted to stay. My boss was compassionate and understanding, yet firm and decisive and so back to Dalaman. I only just missed the first plane out. I got the second. I needed to still my mind so I concentrated on every detail of observation of my fellow passengers.

Chapter Three- The Preparation

As each day had passed he had grown stronger. Each day Baydar senior educated his son into the perils and follies of religion. The crusades, ISIS were easy to grasp. How, in fact, religious authorities had, and were, blinding the hungry and starving and driving them to commit the most awful of atrocities. The heroes of the Crusades, thugs with a red cross in front. Jihadist women in France dying a martyr's death spurred on by an apparently dead Abu Bakr al-BaghDadi. Major news of Saudi women being allowed to drive, because religious freedom or lack of it encroaches at every cultural level. All around the world had been controlled by fear of a divine substance. Logic and intellectualism gave way on a Friday, Saturday or Sunday depending on your religion. And yet for some, the faith was indeed life encapsulating resulting in death. Buddhism in the West had long been in favour but in Myanmar politics and power meant more and ethnic cleansing by Buddhist authorities typified Baydar's evidence on the need for a new age to dawn. "Imagine" was played through the iPod frequently, a song of haunting beauty as it wrestled with life's meaning. Didn't everybody want a better world? No, not everybody. There were those who fought to maintain the status quo.

"I am not saying that the books are wrong. No. There are eternal truths written in them. What I am saying is that those who profess to be adherents of the "book", the word of God, pick and choose the detail and the specifics rather than seeing the big picture, the big story, that is why religion gets reinvented, that is why it never gets to where it should be. Look at the human soul, the human spirit. Look at how much it can achieve. Liberate it, not by confining it to words written two, three, four thousand years ago."

It made sense. He believed. As long as his father didn't found a new movement then he knew it was true. A new movement of people adhering to this way of life wouldn't work. It was an oxymoron. It necessitated one person to initiate the change, the change from within. And that was what he didn't quite understand. Change from within.

By the time of the new tourist season he was ready for the outside world. The management team of the previous year once they were back from holiday all found jobs in hotels that stayed open during the winter months. Baydar took on new staff which suited him. Limited questions. Damir was just another member of staff. The eldest by far but the one who spoke the tourist languages.

It was the eve of Eid al-Adha when his father knocked gently on the door of his room cum chalet. It is time you fulfil your destiny.

Damir looked up. His father in his eighties had been nurturing something but words like destiny seemed a little out of place for a waiter in Kabak.

"Son, the world is full of hate and religion is used and has used people to destroy. It must stop this self destructive movement to Armageddon. The messages of love and peace are ignored, thrown away as fairy tales. In a few weeks you will go to England and you will show them the error of their ways."

Damir guffawed.

The old man look hurt.

"Father, why would they listen to me?"

"They won't listen to you, they will fear you because you will demonstrate just how unsafe they are. You will force them to come together against a common enemy and that enemy will be you. Love is not something that is acceptable in this selfish world. The only way to make them see sense is to drive them to fear, to terrorise them. Their selfishness will ensure they come together to protect, to preserve. You will need to get at the heart of their vulnerability, to destroy their egos and their arrogance. The West is controlled and dominated by people who know nothing will ever happen to them. And the silent majority acquiesce believing also that nothing will happen to them. And yet still people die every day in the most preventable of accidents. The lamentations of Jeremiah and of Rachel must be revisited in this new generation. Christ came claiming that he brought a sword to the world, yet a sword pierced his own mother's soul and a spear stuck into his side after his death. The wailing and gnashing of teeth he foretold was limited to only a few of his disciples and then it changed, as you know. The stories are relevant but only if heard. The stories have been used to further the ends of the few. The importance of them, the strength of them has disappeared. Religion in all its many forms no longer has a place in society. It is irrelevant. Instead let the truths behind the faith that inspired those religions speak volumes. They say that in the West they live in the dawning of a new spiritual age. You are the catalyst to usher in that age. History teaches that civilisations have only responded to fear. Look at the world now. North Korea is left alone to abuse and murder until it becomes a threat, until it has that fear. Mugabe in Zimbabwe is left alone to brutalise his own people and yet some people somewhere still felt it was a good idea for him to be a goodwill ambassador for the WHO as his own health service failed in ignominy. People respond to fear when they feel it will happen to them. You are the lance and this is the boil. You will gain nothing, perhaps you will lose everything. I don't know. You must strike at the heart of their sanctimonious souls. You must strike at the heart of their complacency."

He had finished exhausted. He was a tired old man carrying the world on his shoulders. Demir did not question; he never really had. He accepted the words without comment. He needed to think. So he walked out onto the road and started to run.

By the end of the run he had a plan of action. Baydar senior found him for the evening coffee nightcap. "Father, I need a book on chemistry."

"Yes my son." In that brief exchange all that could be said, all that would be said on the subject, was started, discussed and concluded.

Silence had accompanied the two Baydars through the younger's convalescence, education and training. Thoughts sporadic sprung up in Damir's mind. Memories intruded, flashing across momentarily and then disappearing again into the ether. He remembered having run before, competed even. His father confirmed it. He remembered little girls running around him, growing up. His father confirmed his sisters had been killed in 'the blast'. He remembered English as a language far more than Russian. His father once more acknowledged the memory- "Educated in Cambridge, Chemistry, a First. Proud, so proud your Mother and I." Note-lets of a memory but no cohesion to the single events and faces.

Incoherent memories were flooding as he boarded the plane in Dalaman. He had travelled before, of course he had; Cambridge. But what had happened after Cambridge? He never asked. He never felt he could. Why? The soporific heat was immediately calmed with the blistering air conditioning of the plane, drying his pores out and sucking the life from him. He was healed physically and he felt like a new man but the air conditioning was intolerable. The questions that had started in his head were becoming uncontrollable, deafening. Blast? War? Syria? How many people had he killed? What was going through his father's mind? Theirs had been an unemotional farewell, a transaction of words said formally rather than with meaning. After the blast how did he get to Kabak? Syria was eight hundred miles away? He would have listened! He would have listened, wouldn't he? And would this work? Bringing peace by bringing terror? It didn't make sense. Yet his Dad was so sure, and surely after everything, he owed him? In Kabak when the questions got too much he ran, restoring some kind of equilibrium, punishing his body and freeing his mind. To be sat on a plane, like a sardine in a tin, for the next four hours was an intolerable thought and perhaps an even more intolerable reality.

Further back and to the right a lowly constable from the Metropolitan Police was sat slumped. The world had caught her unawares, unprepared for this side of life. Hers had been a pointless trip. Ruby Greene was being held somewhere in a Turkish prison for supposedly conspiring against the regime. There is no organisation that can be so deaf as those who don't want to hear.

♦

The following day I returned to my desk and saw a standard manila file. There was a hand written note scrawled across the top.

"Ysella. This is sensitive. The case is a domestic dispute. You're not interested in that. Your interest is the case worker. Maybe a safeguarding issue?"

My boss always seemed to insist that safeguarding cases were handled with pen and paper rather than email and computer. He wanted to keep everything cloak and dagger to ensure the guilty weren't given warning.

I left my desk and travelled to a court that I had never seen. The court house was either being prepared for or needed a major makeover. White paint across the semi-circular far wall of the main structure out of which rose a Basilica-esque dome that had seen better days. The building itself was of its time. Not classical, but timeless; yet pretentiously medieval making it obviously twentieth century; late 70's, early 80's.

The suited and booted paraded through its open hallway, carry cases rolling along behind them. Anxious faces of the witnesses and the accused with the cold ones of the barristers and solicitors simply doing their job. There is no such thing as a detached observer. The very walls themselves ooze adrenalin to put everyone on edge. Faces stonewalling other faces, looking down to avoid contact at all costs. The story in my file was of a young lady grieving the loss of her father and found herself a defendant in this court in a case brought forward by her mother. In the one moment when her dad closed his eyes for the last time she lost both her parents. The mother, whom she had known all her life, changed overnight. She became a stranger to her. Her children cut off from their Grandmother. It took a barrister's intervention to establish any kind of communication between them; email. I saw in her face how her whole life had disappeared. I had read about the mother yet even I was shocked when she walked into the court building holding hands with a man. The look across the girl's face said it all. No emotion. No anger. No recognition. The woman in front of her was no longer her mother.

The day at court dragged on. Solicitors and barristers moving between one interview room and the other with brief sojourns into court 4 to update the judge. It continued into the evening at another solicitor's offices. Progress was painful with each word negotiated over. Draft schedule after draft schedule altered with lines, arrows and additional words. It was obvious the girl's relationship with her mother had become a meaningless exercise in negotiation. The memory of her father was what drove her and yet she feared the memories were becoming faint. The memories of her mother had been eradicated through the sight of the woman in front of her being exceedingly and painfully distinct.

It is mundanity, the process of negotiation. Boring, mindless and yet at the same time highly charged and emotional. An oxymoron of life. Hanging around and waiting followed by a sudden flurry of activity and decisions required immediately. The Mont Blanc fountain pen with the Rotary watch danced over the paperwork explaining point by point. The barrister's wedding finger no longer had the ring but the pale circle of flesh betrayed the past. We had been in his presence for twelve hours and the windows at the solicitor's office were misting with condensation.

Magnolia is depressing paint don't you think? It seemed to dominate the office. Office? Small class room representative of a by-gone era in an old university seminar room with high ceilings and fluorescent lighting. The adrenaline was seeping away and tiredness casually entered by the front door. By the time the documents were signed, finally, all were drained. There were no winners, except the pay packet. In the end the signatures were written more through a sense of resignation than with any purpose. The mother had stood there revoking all Last Will and

Testaments including her deceased husband's because it turned out the daughter, the girl I seemed to have befriended, wasn't hers. Even I felt the oblivion enfolding the deep dark pit of despair which was the only emotion on offer. I watched as I saw the young woman physically have the ground of her life removed from below her. There was no foundation left with which she could stand and face the future. There was a void, a nothing, no identity, no meaning to life; she had become overnight a non-existent.

It was perhaps only a matter of days later that I saw her again. This was where I came in; that is the real job. I had casually dropped into the conversation that perhaps it would be good if I could observe the case worker assigned to her case. She readily agreed. "He's creepy." She had shuddered. The case worker was due to arrive at eleven. I arrived at nine.

"It's a lovely name you have," she said as she greeted me at the door of her newly rented flat.

I could hear the crying of the two children that seemed to be incessant and see was visibly drawing her energy inexorably away. She talked as I helped her tidy. Her emotions and life came pouring out. Nappies and toddler clothes bought from charity shops replaced her food. The children were fed and clothed, safe. They weren't happy. She wasn't happy. She didn't know what happiness was. The children's father had left with two words; "I'm out." She had looked up from The Times Crossword that she completed in less than twenty minutes each day, acknowledged his statement and returned to the crossword with a sense of relief. He gave nothing to her, no support during the protracted pre-court negotiations with her estranged mother who wasn't her mother. No money, no support, no nothing. It had been what attracted her to him, he gave nothing, she expected nothing, there was nothing. No arguments. No identity as being a couple, as being a part of something. Two nights of one sided alcohol induced passion after concerts and the family had been conceived. He had stayed because there was no alternative and now she guessed there was. A colleague at work? She didn't know, didn't want to know, didn't care. She didn't even know what his work was. She didn't need to. He had left and nothing had changed. Then she lost her job. The shop, a boutique, had closed and the owner regretfully was retiring to Spain. Would she like to buy it? She would? "But, ah, no! No equity in the property, because it was rented." A rented one bedroomed flat would not act as collateral on the bank loan.

"I'm so sorry my dear, I have to look after number one you know, at my time in life and all that. You must understand, you do understand don't you?"

Another foundation pillar of her life removed. She applied for other positions in other jobs. But they weren't as accommodating of the children and child care was going to cost more than she could earn. Her one luxury in life, the daily Times Crossword became unaffordable. She and the girls went to the library each day and while she was engrossed and satisfied, succeeding where those on greater incomes failed, the children became bored, unruly, unsociable and they were all barred. They went to the park but its equipment was old and broken. They became ensconced at home, the card for the electric left without money for twenty-four hours each time it ran out. The house phone was relinquished. The TV license lapsed, the hire-purchase TV returned. The girls were content but not oblivious. The dark searching eyes struggling to find meaning in life. She had been assigned a family support worker and this was the man over whom hung a large dark cloud of suspicion and conjecture.

At 10.45 a classic MGB GT arrived. I moved myself to the bedroom and observed through the window a smartly dressed older man with a pencil moustache climb out.

I could hear how uncomfortable she was in his presence, apologising for the mess that we had just cleaned up. Apologising for needing support. I sat at an angle so I could see through a crack in the door. I saw him grimace as if he tolerated people. There was no compassion only his duty and something else. There was almost an odour about him and now I felt decidedly uncomfortable. I saw him look her up and down as she turned to call the girls across the living room to him. She caught the look to and I saw in her face the repulsion she felt toward him.

He suddenly turned nasty.

"I'm not good enough for a slut like you? Is that what you think? Well its a bit late now to have some standards, two brats, no husband. Your whoring caught you out didn't it? Well it's the likes of me who decide the fates of sluts like you."

I came out of the bedroom but before I had chance to say anything, he was now alarmed and grabbed my wrist turning me toward him and holding me too close. I smelt last night's whisky on his breath and gagged. This drew his anger and then I felt his arousal just before he punched me. In one moment I was disgusted, frightened and on high alert. My training kicked in and moments later he was on the floor and I was arresting him for assaulting a police officer.

In reality that was my involvement finished. Yet I was left wondering, what would her identity become? How would she define herself? Her children also? I hoped she wouldn't remember his last words to her. Yet the power of words in the fragility of the mind sometimes creates people that don't exist. I did not want her to fulfil his opinion of her, she had to break free from the shackles of wondering who she was and assert herself and recognise the reality of the moment, the moment of her as mother.

Chapter Four- The Beginning of the End

The local newspapers of Clydebank, Sutton Coldfield, Birmingham, Ipswich, Bishop's Stortford, Walthamstow, High Wycombe, Slough and Sutton all carried a similar headline.

"Explosion outside local Cinema." It was only because there was a similar explosion in London's Haymarket did the national Press take interest and then there was an explosion of activity in itself across the Met, the local constabularies and the media.

My boss had realised that I had come back from Turkey a bit disjointed and then thrust into the safeguarding case immediately which in turn was immediately taken out of my hands. Suddenly I realised that the anniversary of my dad's death had passed. The first anniversary and still no answers. I was low. So I was assigned as the Met's representative working with the other affected forces to try to get to the bottom of these explosions. All the cinemas were from the same chain- Empire, so it was pretty obvious it was a disaffected employee or a crackpot with some kind of axe to grind. Not all the "Empires" were affected. The obvious question was, was that deliberate? Or were there unexploded devices or was there another reason?

Each Forensics Department was analysing the kind of device. Crackpot or not, this was well planned and well executed except no-one was killed, hurt or maimed. These were low key explosives and went off just as the staff were locking up, or thereabouts on the very same evening. I was working on the presumption that it was a group with planning and knowledge.

There was a quick meeting and a press conference. I had to take a call and it was during that forty second interval that I was elected as the Met's representative to the press conference. I had done the training but this would be my first one. I ran through the phrases in my head and jotted them down.

"No firm leads at the moment." "We are continuing with our enquires." "Joint task force across the country." "No idea of motive." "No one had taken responsibility." "People across the country should stay calm and be vigilant." "Anything out of the ordinary should be reported immediately to your local police force."

It was bland. Not really newsworthy. Then I was asked one question by a journalist from a tabloid.

"So, do you think this is an anti-capitalist plot designed to overthrow the Establishment?"

A question out of nowhere.

"Uhh, well I think this is more thoughtful than that. This is someone or some ones trying to make a point that they could kill if they wanted to."

The journalist sent across another salvo, "What would be the point in that?"

I engaged in dialogue rather than following my training.

"It is a warning shot. A sign perhaps to ourselves to mend our ways, not be too cocky, don't take life for granted." What on earth was I saying. I was making it up, yet it was what I believed. This is how I saw it. It was planned to every detail. There was no coincidence here. It wasn't though thought out, logical or rational. It was gut instinct. The stuff of Hollywood movies or Rankin novels, not real life in the Met.

Of course this is what shot across the papers and created more turmoil. My bosses were furious, "She'll never do a press conference again."

"Who the hell does she think she is? Dostoevsky?"

Life can be lonely when you stick your neck out and become real. It isn't safe and you soon see who your friends are. It looked like I had perilously few. I knew it meant nothing. MI5 would be taking everything over and my brief sortee into the press would be a two minute wonder, quite literally.

A bomb went off in a dustbin outside of Sainsbury's in Brighton. For the townsfolk it sent shudders back to the dark days of Tebbit and Thatcher and the Brighton of 12th October 1984 when the provisional IRA, and in particular Patrick Magee, tried to kill the Prime Minister and her Cabinet as they stayed in the Grand Brighton Hotel for the Conservative Party conference that year. How could it happen again? Mercifully no-one was hurt. Just like the "Empire Bombings" which had made the British public decidedly uncomfortable. The Empire Chain were giving away tickets at buy one get one free to try to change the obvious downturn in sales. Forensics were now working round the clock so the Brighton report was only hours after the explosion itself. According to the report, it was a small home-made bomb wrapped in cling film so that sniffer dogs wouldn't detect it. It used a combination of ammonium nitrate and nitromethane and if it was meant to hurt it failed miserably. Broughton of MI5 read the report. He sat there ponderously looking out at the night sky burning more electricity than the country of Nepal. It wasn't what the report said, it was pretty bland, it was what was left out. He picked up the phone and rang the laboratory.

"I want you to come and see me please............Yes now."

♦

Ten minutes later the author of the report was before him explaining the infinite detail. Broughton, his eyes rolling back into the sockets, eventually lost the will to live.

"I know what it is, I know what you've written, I want to know what you THINK!"

"Ah, well that's the interesting bit," the scientist continued. "I think it was meant to be this way, meant not to hurt, meant just to frighten. And by choosing Brighton......."

He was cut off. "It wouldn't take much to re-kindle the dealings of fear and terror. Yes I see, yes I see." Broughton was murmuring to himself really. "Ok, that's enough. Goodbye."

"And of course with the Empire bombings does anyone really feel safe anymore?"

"That is enough." The scientist was getting on his nerves by disturbing his train of thought.

The scientist shifted uncomfortably and imperceptibly to Broughton whose mind was lost in another reality. The goal of terrorism is fear. It doesn't necessarily have to be much. A small bomb on the Brighton seafront, a town metaphorically of dried kindling wood to which the smallest match would make an impact. That, after the firelighters of the Empire bombings had already been placed. There was your highly charged propaganda machine which the British press would just devour. But from the terrorists, here was a statement. What was the aim? Political, religious or ideological, he mused. Political? The Brexit from Europe was more boring than highly charged. A cabinet minister had even been quoted that the "Brexit negotiations are enough to drive anyone to look forward to the LibDem annual conference." Society, even the maverick hardline, had really given up on getting any meaningful understanding let alone decisions. The question of Northern Ireland was not settled, yet the will to kill had lessened. Religious? He screwed his eyes up and pulled his hands through his hair. His glasses came off as they always did so when he felt under stress. Something, something was different. He started muttering. Brighton was not really high profile. The Empire towns, except for the Haymarket, weren't either. And the Haymarket was just the end of the theme. If IS or its supporters in this country really wanted to create terror they would hit a liberal mosque, or Number Ten, or Westminster. Broughton bolted upright.

"What day is it?"

The scientist had almost escaped but stuck his bag through the door still ajar.

"Monday."

"So it exploded yesterday."

"Yes, Sunday at zero nine hundred hours; it's all in my report." The scientist was exasperated.

The fact that there was no response, the scientist took as his cue to leave the office. This time faster than before.

Broughton mused. Why would someone place a small explosive outside a supermarket when it was virtually empty. Just a few staff but no customers. Why? The staff would hear and report, thus ensuring fear would spread like wild fire. But no injuries, not even a broken window. This was ideological. Maximum of fear, terror, but actually no injuries for which to feel guilt. It was a message, a sign and powerful one at that. This had to be taken seriously. It was too powerful a statement but he feared his superiors would make him file under "Pending." No loss of life, no injuries. Therefore under the Explosive Substances Act 1883 it would be difficult to get life imprisonment for the perpetrator because it was obvious it was there not to endanger life. But if caught with the ingredients, like Faris Al-Khori, the perpetrator could get time inside for possession. Clever? Dangerous? The affects of terrorism can throw a country into meltdown. Vigilante groups are established, trust disappears. Your neighbours become suspects, especially if the tabloid-reading public are fuelled by their papers. But what was the ideology? To know that would be to catch the perpetrator.

An email blinked onto his computer screen.

"Yesterday's bombing. We are leaving it to the Sussex police force. We've given them the suspects on our radar but whoever it was didn't know what they were doing, so nothing to worry about."

The frustration welled up in Broughton's face as he reddened with rage.

"Idiots," he shouted. This was too clever. It couldn't be ignored, he was sure of that. But if he wasn't allowed to do the spade work, he needed someone who could. Tomorrow he would be interviewing for a new member of the team. That would be as normal. Now he would also be interviewing for a secondment, a placement to gain experience. Someone outside of MI5, someone eager to please so they would keep quiet but experienced enough to get some answers. He thumbed through the files. Two candidates looked really strong to join the team, the third looked interesting. Umm, perhaps a liability, would need a firm controlling hand, but tenacious, able to work alone, able to follow leads in private. Ysella Mae, a high flyer but too young really for the team. She needed more experience, yet for the past year she had been in her own time investigating the disappearance, assumed death, of her father. Just the candidate. "Sorry girl, you won't be joining MI5, I have a more interesting job for you. And it looks like you are already involved." He glanced at the television with Ysella's face at the press conference.

"Now who's your boss?" he said audibly. "Oh, good." He smiled genuinely as his eyes scanned a familiar name. He got up, relaxed now, and walked down the stairs to go home.

♦

The call from the Met was 5.30 in the morning. I was being seconded to MI5. Had my application been successful? No, the interview was today, but that now apparently was cancelled. Strange. I was to report to a man called Broughton. That is all I knew. I did know that this was a significant change. Everything around me that I knew, my blankets of protection, my office, my colleagues, were all changing in a sudden phone call and not the phone call I had envisaged or worked for. This was out of my comfort zone.

Aristotle believed that courage is the most important quality. The 'Cowardly Lion' who followed the Yellow Brick Road found the courage within him for it is within us, more specifically it is in the subgenual anterior cingulate cortex. Therefore it is possible for us to train our minds to face adversity with courage. Much as we train our bodies to compete at sport, or we train our minds to solve crosswords, so we can with courage. When this is perfected with evidenced based neurological research, the world of treating anxiety disorders will be changed forever. It is not just about facing fear it is about living with risk and uncertainty. All of us in varying ways, for varying times live with elements of risk in our lives. As Ernest Hemingway put it, "courage is grace under pressure." And we can adapt ourselves. Unfortunately our understanding of religion, and the religious language and symbols that we use, can often contradict our ability to train our minds. Firstly we must be vulnerable. Brent Brown has found that belief in our own unworthiness ensures that we live in fear based lives. Religious liturgy, especially Christian liturgy, is full of sentences like "we are not worthy to receive", or "the confession". Dad struggled with being reminded daily that he was a 'sinner'. He taught me, though, that actually, God created us who we are, and loves us for who we are, an original blessing. We have an incarnational theology which means we believe God values and loves us. By doing the "I am unworthy," we bow our heads in self protection instead of being vulnerable and saying to ourselves, "What is the worst that can happen?" Brown says courage and vulnerability are closely aligned and having both increases the quality of our lives. That means we must dare to fail- because actually what are we in fear of? I am therefore clearly a product of my mum and dad.

We have to acknowledge our fears, that means being honest with ourselves and understanding what we are afraid of. Only then can we be courageous. Honesty should not beget judgement but frequently and ashamedly it does.

And of course we therefore have to ensure we have the opportunity to conquer our fears by exposing ourselves to them. For instance if we fear failing at a job interview, the only way to conquer that fear is to go for a job interview. Not that MI5 gave me the chance. When we fail we realise that it isn't as bad as we feared and therefore will have courage to do it again. Failure is not something that our religion would embrace. Inasmuch as I have a religion. Shusaku Endo writes of the most despicable men who sin again and again and yet he demonstrates that God's love is for them, and more so for them. If we think positively one day we may well get that job; certainly we all know that thinking negatively can often mean we fulfil our thoughts. There are sports psychologists the world over who make a living out of training their sports clients to visualise winning. By visualising what we can achieve and then acting on it we will conquer our fears and anxiety. Yet Christianity in particular can confuse that thinking positively negates the grace of God. This is why despite feeling the faith I can't go to Church. I can't stand the thought of listening to banal tripe handed down by the spoon-load as if I had no thought of my own.

So how do we reconcile the scientific evidence-based research of psychologists with our, "well perhaps then I am Christian", religion? This isn't the age of enlightenment when religion is seen as either an ethical framework or superstitious nonsense on the one hand or the ultimate word of God on the other. Suddenly we believe that in all things science and religion we can encounter God, and it is those encounters we try to provide for all, and in those encounters open ourselves to God's love and grace. We therefore have to reconcile these seemingly mutually exclusive positions. Yep, I can hear my father.

He spoke of the story of Jesus meeting the demoniac. The demoniac's first words to Jesus, other than recognising who he was, are- "Do not torment me." Basically, leave me alone, I am afraid for the future to risk any change. The townsfolk came out to see what happened and saw the change in the demoniac and were afraid. Change- fear of the unknown. And then that fear spread.

The ex-demoniac wanted to stay with Jesus, because anything else was fearful and would have caused great anxiety. Essentially he would have replaced one crutch for another, but Jesus sent him away to find the courage to face his fears by ensuring the ex-demoniac was exposed to those fears. Fear pervades this story. Fear, the basis of terrorism. God in the story is recognised not only in the compassion but also in the challenge to conquer the legion of fears which assailed him. God throughout the Bible from Abraham to Jonah, to Jesus and Paul inspires humanity to take some responsibility- Jesus said, "Sin no more," to the threatened woman. He said, "Sell all you have," to the rich man. Jesus saw in the demoniac the vulnerability but did not say, "You are unworthy"; he said "What is your name?" "Who are you?" And we are called to be honest and say this is me, God, and Jesus released the man from his demons and our honesty releases us. We are no longer afraid and we then allow the grace of God to work within us. It isn't about either God's grace or our humanity, it is about both. If our humanity wasn't important and it was purely God's grace then we wouldn't need the theology of the incarnation that says God dwells within us. If it was just God's grace then it could be zapped down from above. Rather, it is God's grace for our humanity that means we should have courage and not be afraid, and respond to Jesus' challenge to the ex-demoniac to return home and declare how much God has done. For the ex-demoniac, who had legions of demons leave him, was more grateful than those who had just one demon for as in the Jesus parable, the more we are forgiven the greater our faith.

Faith should teach us that to be vulnerable, honest and acknowledge our fears releases us from them, and it teaches us that we cannot hide from them behind Jesus. Rather, actually that very same Jesus sent people like us away to conquer those fears. What Jesus taught does not contradict modern science, instead gives a narrative to the new discoveries. Religion lets faith down. My dad's inner struggle is my struggle and yet still each Sunday I stole away to an early morning mass just to sit and be mindful of the preciousness of life.

Dressed in dungarees I left my aunt and uncle's house in Brighton. They had both left for work earlier than I had needed to rise.

By car, Sainsbury's was only five minutes away, I decided to walk. I wasn't sure what I was supposed to be looking for but Broughton had not wanted to come himself so I might as well take the opportunity to clear my head. Even walking briskly it seemed to take an age to get there. The wind blowing off the coast wrapped my hair around my face at every opportunity. Even as a child I had never minded the hair in my face. Sainbury's was open. Forensics had scoured the area and found nothing. They had checked the video footage outside of the store for the previous twenty fours before the detonation and seen nothing. It was my job to spot what they hadn't. Needle in a haystack time.

The manager, a middle aged lady, was obviously on tenterhooks. She had a hairstyle reminiscent of "Crystal Tips and Alistair" from my childhood. Her over-anxious handshake was cold and sweaty. In the video room I asked for the footage of the detonation to be replayed backwards. The bin was in the bottom right hand corner of the screen because the camera was set up looking at the car park. Seeing in slow motion the bin apparently repair itself made my flesh shudder. I don't know why, but down the spine tiny beads of perspiration formed. I leaned forward in the chair pretending I was interested, pretending that I could spot even the smallest of details that no-one else would ever see.

Time is a fascinating instrument for humanity. Time is essentially meaningless except for the context it is set within. The last five minutes of a football game when your team are one nil up but with their backs to the wall takes an eternity. And yet watching a film which captivates you, time flies by. Sitting watching the monitors that morning, time was inexorably slow. I was just about struggling to keep my eye-lids open and if I had been driving would have wound down the window when I saw a familiar face.

"STOP".

The controller paused the frame. "Go back a bit." I exhaled. "There, him."

"Ok, I see a shopper with four hessian bags, shopping at Sainsbury's." The controller's sarcasm got on my nerves.

"I've seen him before."

"Probably a local, you've probably seen him in the bank queue."

"But I'm not local. Look we have nothing to go on so far, we might as well follow some kind of lead."

"Dead end more like."

"Find him when he is entering the shop, not leaving."

The tape reeled back a lot faster. The man, mid- late 50's ish was fit for his age had entered the store thirty five minutes before. The handles of his hessian bags were all coming out of one bag in the way all shoppers do. There was nothing unusual, the controller was right about that but I knew I had seen him before, but where? I got the controller to go back to when the man left the shop. Counted four bags. Reeled forward once more to him entering the shop. I counted the bag handles again. there were five bags on entering. Four on leaving and each bag was jammed with groceries. A fifth bag would have been used by logical people in such circumstances.

The controller was getting interested now, maybe excited. He zoomed and panned out as much as the equipment would allow. The playback was slowed to .1 of a second interval delays, and there slowly and quietly, it was. A hessian bag being placed in the bin in a fraction of a second. We ran forward again to when the man entered. We zoomed in on the bag and though it was nothing concrete, it certainly looked like the bag that held the other four bags and something more in it. An undefinable shape.

I grabbed the forensic report from my back pack and scanned through, excitedly. It clearly stated traces of hessian were spread around the area. Nothing of interest if written by someone who didn't do shopping. Who, out shopping, places a hessian bag in a bin? Their whole point is reusability. Not a crime but certainly bizarre. It was the face though that had sparked my interest. Where I had seen him. He was tanned or Mediterranean. His clothes fitted well. I saw an emblem I recognised.

"Scan in on the jeans."

"What am I looking for?"

"That label," I said pointing a finger inanely.

"Legato."

"Turkish. That's where I've seen him, he was on the flight from

Dalaman with me."

"Can you be sure?"

"Yes, look at the healed scarring around the neck and hands. I studied every passenger in the airport to keep my mind….active."

"What, you think he's some kind of injured fighter with IS from Syria?"

"I don't know, but that is our man, the man from Dalaman. I've got to call this in."

Broughton was interested but not enthusiastic. "I want a name."

"Yes sir."

Brighton to Gatwick is but a hop, skip and a jump and I made the calls as I walked back to my car on Bennett Road. I was met by the Head of Security and Passport Control and it didn't take long because of course I knew which plane, which terminal and the face to find the man with the hessian bags in Brighton. Thirty minutes later having slurped some disgusting instant coffee, I was out of the building heading back to London with a name.

Living and parking in London is not easy and because of the transport system I had no need to keep my car where I lived. Instead I had a garage just outside the congestion zone in Putney. I rented the garage by the month, my thinking being that one day I may decide to sell the car and just use public transport. That day had not yet come. Because of the traffic that I did not want to endure I grabbed the Gatwick Express and was heading toward Milbank less than an hour later. The car could be collected overnight. For now I had adrenaline pumping through my body. I had decided not to ring Broughton on the train. Too public. Instead I scanned my eyes just in case. The man from Dalaman wasn't to be seen. It was stupid to think he would be.

"Damir Baydar."

"And you are sure? Yes of course you are! Right. I want everything on him. But don't make too much noise about this. I'll contact a friend in Interpol; see if she has anything." He was matter of fact which did not resonate well with my excitement. I felt a little deflated. My first assignment to which I can been mysteriously seconded. I had done everything asked of me. A smile. A congratulations. A well done would not have gone amiss. But he wanted more.

"Ok," I said. I returned to my desk and set to work. Broughton would only want the essentials. An hour later a summary was placed on his desk.

"Damir Baydar, Kurdish son of a Mujahideen commander. Kept from Afghanistan by his mother who sent him to Cambridge. A Chemistry first and return to Turkey. Became a Chemist in Turkey until his mother was murdered by an IS bomb bringing Father out of retirement and exile. Together father and son fought against IS in Syria. Three years ago he had been ambushed, presumed kidnapped and presumed dead. The Father, an extremely old man was heartbroken, disappeared. Could speak several languages passably. Blood Type 0. No known distinguishing marks."

"Thank you." Broughton began. "Now, London St Pancras for you. My contact in Interpol thinks the Paris Gendarmerie may have something."

Chapter Five- Now we see in a mirror, darkly

I took a detour across London. I don't know why I felt ultra cautious, perhaps over anxious, but I didn't want to be linked to MillBank. Instead I became camouflaged with the tourists and families from the West descending on Paddington. I, though, wasn't phased by the single change at Edgware Road where it seemed all trains stopped only to walk the five metres across the platform and immediately onto the Circle Line running in the same direction. Logically it didn't make sense. Logic had ceased to become important in a world of reality.

On entering the terminus at St. Pancras one is transcended at once into a quintessentially twenty-first century Britain in a Victorian Shell.

There is something about the cosmopolitan nature of the passengers that makes a simple train journey an experience to be savoured. The predominance of the accentuated French accents, American drawl, guttural German and overtly refined English, predominate the carriage. The strong accents of Liverpool, the black country, Yorkshire and Essex are missing. For some reason, a strange reason, this alongside the view of overhead wires makes the journey feel different. Or maybe it is just that we, me and my fellow travellers who look up in acknowledgement as you try to ease by, or look down as you try to ease some room for them, are travelling to France. It is something in the mind, the knowledge that determines the feeling. The head influences the heart. Logic determines emotion maybe? I know I am travelling to France and therefore does this make it an exciting journey? Would it be the same if I was travelling to, say, Ashford? Not that there is anything wrong with Ashford. You barely see it from the Eurostar. But it doesn't hold the same emotional appeal as say, and purely as an example, Paris.

The end result, it seems, determines the nature of the journey. A spiritual journey therefore can be all the more positive if the end is known or expected. A spiritual journey that only has death as its reward is depressing and possibly short. There is something about the end. There is also something about the nature of the journey. It can be endured or it can enjoyed. You can close your eyes and plug the headphones in or you can open the bottle of Prosecco, enjoy the toddler across the gangway and live the moment. Who brings painting for a child to do on the Eurostar? The middle aged parents of this toddler who enthralled the carriage and captivated us. The mother was a genius. Yes a little mess but a contented child who kept us entertained for the whole two hours and sixteen minutes. The blond pigtail shining as she frequently turned on her mother's lap seeking the matriarchs approval. Enjoy this precious moment. Or endure it. To endure is not to like, to see the playfulness and be antagonised. Yet a toddler with paint is a teacher with a book, an analyst with their smart-phone, a student with their lover, a non-executive director with chinos and Jimmy Choo's complemented with a Longines on their left wrist. Natural at oneness. Exuding contentment.

The journey is part of the experience. The holiday starts with the journey not with the arrival else you wish your life away. So much can be enjoyed on the way. The orchards of Kent like a thought, story or PHD hold such promise of a land of unknown pleasures. One source and a variety of outcomes and pleasures: apple sauce, cider or simply an apple. Whatever the future may hold they all come from the same beginning. Like the concept of an idea; where will it lead us today? As such you can't have the end necessarily in sight. There may be an inkling of where it would all end, but that isn't important. Because the journey could take us anywhere, we could have our eyes opened to new possibilities. That is how great scientific advances are discovered. It is the realm of dreams and childlike exploration. Theology loses out on this journey by determining the end- Nirvana, heaven, Armageddon, re-incarnation. Theology loses out. The end justifies the means, and the journey is lost to endurance. It is therefore to be endured. To be tolerated. Such a shame. Sit for a while on a train, open your eyes to the abundance of life in all its richness and let it determine your spiritual journey wherever it may lead.

I sat there and my shoulder throbbed. The acceptance of life and putting up with its inadequacies is part of humanity's make-up. We adapt and get by. To a lesser or greater extent this is true. The desire to live at all costs. To achieve. To thrive. To overcome. It's part of the human condition. We don't lie down and take it. Yet those who do, who are weighed down, tired of the trials of life, who can't fight and adapt any more, are left behind. Life has been a struggle to get up in the morning let alone to get to work. Maybe it takes all the energy simply to get the children ready for school. They leave the garden gate, hanging off its hinges, behind and one is left alone to descend into a pit only to drag oneself out on hearing the footsteps and chatter back down the garden path seven hours later. Alcohol, drugs, pills, overwork, gaming addiction, can mask the pain.

I arrived in the eleventh arrondissement, the Bastille area. Hippy, trendy, fashionable boutiques interspersed with cafes and bars. The street, at the T junction of which my apartment was, was a bar-lined student paradise. Transvestites, swingers, LGBT, straights, families of every colour and culture predominated this enclosed street no more than ten feet wide. Cars waited and moved gently, patiently edging forward between the throngs of people who good-naturedly moved aside on the sudden realisation that in slow motion they were to be mowed down.

Some of the metro in Paris is modernised with its double decker carriages moving thousands at any given moment across France's capital. Often trains still required the handle to open the door, families are respected, the pushchair provoking an Old Testament style parting of the sea. Finding in the city of love a particular place that epitomises love is impossible. The Arc de Triomphe on the busiest roundabout in Europe is not known for its charm. The walk down the Champs-Elysees though, reminiscent of a wider and more spacious Oxford Street, was enchanting in itself. To get swallowed within an atmosphere on enculturated love head for Montmatre. Climb the steps to the Sacre-Coeur and then swing left to the artist's square with its eateries and hawkers. Some artists genuinely selling their own work, others selling Chinese imports that the unsuspecting American public unknowingly exclaim, "Oh darling! I've just got to have that, it is 'sooooo' French." No bartering or haggling but feeling all the time that they have got that part of Paris to take back to the US and all for forty euros and a one dollar import. Everybody leaves at the end of the day happy. Capitalism at its best providing instant gratification. Within a stone's throw, the Sacre-Coeur has not escaped consumerism. Alongside the boards requesting silence at every turn are the electronic medal making machines in honour of St. Michael, Jean-Paul II and every other Catholic you could name.

The view from the base of the Sacre Coeur does not take in the Eiffel Tower yet if you just meander to your right and slightly down the hill it is there, through the railings, in all its majesty. I took a picture, because you do, don't you? I felt drawn to it so I took the metro to Bir-Hakeim. It was a long journey, or at least should not have been. Only after twenty minutes did I eventually clock that I was on the wrong line. In my mind I had struggled with the metro map and eventually worked out a long-winded but less tortuous route back. You can't come to Paris without viewing the Tower I persuaded myself. So an hour later than was necessary I arrived to see the gardens being refurbished and a long queue even at 6pm, I looked up, saw the massive piece of Meccano and left. I was underwhelmed.

I returned to the Eleventh Arrondissement and sat there, Temperanillo in hand. I should have given Mum a call, maybe she could have met me. Maybe though I just needed time alone. I ate the plat du jour as I was accustomed. It was Mum's standard fare and advice. "When in France eat the plat du jour." We girls had, having had this drummed into us from an early age. Even on my first trip to France with her, sat on her knee on the ferry crossing, I was eating something from the plat du jour. Smaller portions of the same fare. I may not have had the steak tartare but I did enjoy the Côte d'Agneau, with my tomatoes surreptitiously appearing on my father's plate. Always with wine or beer and frequently both. Me that is, not my father. As my parents and grandparents and sisters drank I would exclaim, at a tender age, "Share" and grasp the aforementioned alcohol and consume. "Share" meant "mine". The latter, I had learnt, didn't get me anywhere whereas the former produced the desired result. At one in the morning the Paris night-life, even mid-week, only now settles. Nightclubs are still partying hard but the restaurants and bars are closing for the night. I found a small bar that unusually served Irish coffee. I remember on more than one occasion Mum had lamented that in her preference for brandy the French paradoxically hadn't yet discovered French coffee. The abhorrence of this English nightcap not even the Eurostar had managed to smuggle across international boundaries. I was left with my thoughts. "What was I to learn tomorrow? Anything? Nothing? Who was I searching for? There was something that was unclear, call it gut instinct. Something about Baydar's journey? Could he be searching for himself?"

The problem with identity, how we identify one-self, is that actually in the large majority of criteria how we do identify ourselves is in relation to others. Our parents, our culture, our religion, our creed. The latter two my dad used to say could be distinct.

I breakfasted alone. I had dressed simply in trousers and jumper and looked more French than the French. My knowledge of the language was passable and when I tried I had enough of an accent to blend in. To blend in? Identity is individualistic and yet we try so often to conform. The distinction between individuality and corporateness is often blurred. My father was at one and the same time applauded and criticised for his individuality. We like people to be different for entertainment but we prefer them to be the same in reality. Who am I? Am I defined by my job? Language? Thoughts? Clothes? Family? Faith? Which is more important; how I see myself or how others see me? The former should be the answer but if the truth be told the latter is often the basis of how we live our lives. Public perception, we know deep down, is unreal yet it still doesn't change the fact how others view us is intrinsically important to our mental health and well being. Continuously we try to conform, adapting to what we know deep inside is the eternal struggle. It is far better, we know, to accept truth and like ourselves for who we are. Yet our identity is so often tied up with how others see us.

I met my colleague in the French Gendarmerie for an hour. It was a pointless exercise. I left. Neither of us was any the wiser. I made my way to the Gard du Nord. Waited. Boarded the Eurostar back to St. Pancras via Ebbsfleet. An hour and a half after leaving the Gard du Nord the Eurostar began the slow approach to the tunnel.

To those reading their magazines or Kindles, watching their tablets or laptops, the change is indiscernible as they continued transfixed. The windows show reflections of people they barely know in reality, themselves. Who are we? Really?

I must have drifted off whilst pondering and before I really woke up I was getting off the Tube finding my way to the office, which was almost full when I arrived. Jenkins was the only person from the team missing and he strode into the room interrupting.

"Sir you need to read this." He passed over the Evening Standard and Broughton unfolded it to the front page headline.

"Dalaman Dan!"

Broughton sighed, "O sweet mother of God." A catholic upbringing is never truly lost. He looked at me, "The security camera controller at Sainsbury's no doubt." A hastily organised press conference was convened. Jenkins read out the prepared statement confirming no facts. No questions were allowed. The ravenous wolves did not get their sacrificial lamb today.

I spent the next couple of weeks following up every possible lead and just as I was beginning to think that Broughton would send me back a letter appeared in the Independent. Not that all letters that are written to a national broadsheet make the front page: this one did, four days after it was received. The editor, too long in the tooth not to ensure its validity, sat on it until he was convinced. Then he opened up a can of worms.

"Dear people of Great Britain. A great country which enabled me to be educated. You are blindly occupying your own lives and not seeing a bigger picture. Not seeing how you can in no small way together change the world. Instead you are maintaining the status quo by enabling war to happen in thirty three places around the world. Your defence budget, against countries and terror that cripples you, is larger than your health budget. Yet terror is cheap and simple to enact. No amount of nuclear submarines can stop what I have done. Wake up people. Smell the coffee. That is all I want to do. To demonstrate to you how easy terror is. Change your ways. Don't involve yourselves with wars all over the world. You look to your gods and your prophets and claim a moral high ground that is dividing your United Kingdom. Think about it. Open your eyes you normal people, brainwashed into accepting that which you are told. You have let your religion and culture set you apart from others. The world is small. Together we can make it work, isolated we destroy it. Religion is not the way to solve problems. It gives a 'them and us' scenario. It is then used as an excuse for war. Take away the excuse you take away any semblance of legitimacy that may have existed. War is not the way to solve problems, on whatever scale. There is always a projected enemy, a projected problem of the moment whether it be Saddam Hussein or Robert Mugabe or Kim Jong-Un. That moment changes though. Hussein is a hero against the Ayatollah. Then he becomes the problem armed by us. The evil of the situation made manifest is important in the moment. We cannot stand by, yet we cannot assume that all the world's problems will be solved with the removal of the leader of the moment. Removing Kim Jong-Un will not make the world totally safe, it will only remove one of the problems, not all of them. History teaches, but we have yet to learn, that there are no victors in war, only survivors. We should all fear the point where there maybe no alternative, hoping that all other alternatives may be worked through first. We need to live in a state where all, politicians included, admit our own frailties in that no one has all the facts to hand. Recognise that we are at the mercy of the tabloids who have neglected to inform the country of the facts that don't suit their agenda. Did you know that when Saddam Hussein came to power he brought in widespread sweeping reform that included more religious freedom than ever before. We must fear a tide of opinion that seeks reparation and revenge when religious minorities could be targeted and scapegoated across the world. And it is the already struggling areas of the world that will be worst hit. We need to ensure that we have our eyes open especially to that which we don't want to see. We cannot turn away our eyes from those countries who commit murder in the name of state security. Whether that country be Palestine or Israel, Iran or Iraq, Turkey, America or Britain, we have to join together, work together against all that confronts true peace and hope. These are gifts that should be universal, not just for the few. We cannot be arrogant enough to equate peace and hope with democracy. How dare any country believe that it has the political system by which all countries should be measured. Democracy is a danger for minorities. Democracy appeals to the selfishness of the individual which politicians tap into. Think about your own system here in Britain. Parliament is made up of two Houses, one elected, one not. Which, therefore, can afford to hold the nation's long term interest at heart? Which has to make popular laws to ensure re-election? Those who stand together for peace whilst supporting those who are forced to defend, together stand for a better world. A world that is just around the corner if only we would seize our chance to grasp it. We cannot go on living in our own little bubble turning a blind eye to the slow erosion of life around us. All I want to do is wake you up out of your golden slumbers. Don't be afraid to carry the weight of bringing in a new world. Else we will all sleepwalk to The End. I am only trying to get you to return to that place you should never have left, helping you to return home if you like. I am only the wake up call. Politics is too important to be left to the politicians."

I laid the paper down and looked at Broughton. "Find him," was all he said.

I had a thought and yet did not vocalise it, replying instead, "Okay." I left the office, bag and coat in tow. It was the proverbial long-shot but I had nothing to lose except a bit of a walk and negotiating the underground. It took seven minutes on the Jubilee line to St John's Wood from Westminster and a further ten to walk to the Abbey Road studios. I was brought up on the Beatles. Abbey Road, the final Beatles album to be recorded, though Let it Be was released the following year. Abbey Road was a happy work, a work that brought that warring Beatles together, united on an album that epitomised their individuality yet gave them a corporate identity. It was their unity album. No hiding away in the pseudonyms of Sgt. Pepper or the out and out feuding of the Double White Album. This brought the creative differences of the Beatles together. Is it a coincidence that Lennon's track "Come Together" opens the album? Toward the end of the album is one track of three songs, demonstrating this coming together. The three song, one track, that had sparked my attention as I read the letter from Baydar was 'Golden

Slumbers/Carry That Weight/The End'. Surely his ideological stance and the aura of the Abbey Road album were synonymous. So I found myself in NW8 wondering what to do next. I stood looking at iconic zebra crossing at a loss. I turned around so my back was towards it and on my left there was a public refuse bin. Worth a chance? Reaching up inside I found an envelope taped to the lid. Adrenaline mixed with excitement and the desire to find an answer is a toxic combination and my training told me to wait before opening it. Rules are there to be broken are they not? Mum had that trait in her. My Dad did not find it that easy. Not that he didn't break the rules, he just wallowed in the depths of despair before, during and after. I stared at the paper which was a mobile phone number, then the training kicked in and I retraced my steps to Thames House.

Chapter Six- The End of the Beginning

"So, ring or text?" Broughton threw open the question to us his team.

"Ring." Phoenix Jenkins liked things just so. "We can identify where he is very quickly."

"Text," Luke Grantham responded. "Just to be disagreeable," he smiled at Jenkins.

"Look," I started, "here is a thoughtful guy, who cares."

"That's it then, text," stated Broughton. "She's getting soft and we don't want a phone conversation going wrong."

"Hello" I texted.

"Hello, and who might you be?" pinged the response.

I looked to Broughton, who looked as if he didn't know the answer and then nodded assent.

"Ysella."

"The young woman of the police who led the press conference?"

"Yep."

There was nothing then. I stared at the phone. I typed.

"You can't bring peace, by bringing war."

"Augustine thought so."

"Who?" Apparently Phoenix Jenkins was good at his job, in delivering just the right report at the right time to the right person, but thinking out of the box was beyond him.

Liam Wilson, the quietest member of the team. He barely spoke, was always guarded as if he never wanted to get anything wrong.

"Augustine, the Emperor who ruled Rome, that's where we get the month of August from."

"That's Caesar Augustus, moron." I exhaled as I turned on my heals and strode toward the desk I had been given. It was harsh and probably set Wilson back a couple of years. As soon as I said it I tried to eat my words. I saw his face, crestfallen. I'd have to make it up to him one day somehow. Not now. Now I was placing myself into an uncomfortable situation from which words could be judged harshly, from which the reactions could be catastrophic.

I needed space to think. We had to get to this guy and quickly. Panic causes good people to take the law into their own hands and vigilante groups were being formed. Anti-religion, anti-anti religion. Anti Muslim, anti Christian. Anti anything. This wave of mayhem precipitated by a few devices that had killed no one. Yet no one felt safe. The ultimate in terror. To what end? To get rid of religion? Was that it? I was unsure. My dad had always taught me that the problem with all the changes that had happened to religion was that they had always re-invented themselves to be worse than the evil they purported to get rid of. It was a basic philosophy but ran simply thus- Judaism was replaced by Christianity, Christianity challenged by Islam. The Catholic Church had to reform itself in defence from the threat posed by the Protestant network of faiths. All Christian Churches of denomination replaced by the "Free" Churches that in themselves had just as many rules and regulations as the Churches they spoke out against. People were the problem. People are the problem.

"People," I found myself muttering.

"What's that?"

"She's just talking to herself, we're not at her intellectual level to be deigned to be spoken to boss."

I heard the sniggers, the cynicism, the envy.

"People," I muttered again and this time cast a glance to the rest of the room. I liked them, but I was discovering they could get on my nerves. Ignorance was not something I easily tolerated. Something I inherited from my mum. I needed to speak to her, I needed to talk, but life's circumstances just got in the way. She was still working. Private clients visiting her from all over Europe. Since my dad had gone she had moved to Fontainebleau, south of Paris and found herself to be a European wide psychologist earning the big money that seemed all too pointless now my dad wasn't there.

I returned my gaze to the phone.

"Just war?"

"Precisely". "Talk?"

"You want to meet?" My fingers were getting numb in the excitement.

"It ain't going to be that easy"

"No I guess not" My mood sobered up rapidly.

"Before we start, just so you know, this isn't to do with Eleanor its more like Michelle"

"Excuse me?"

"Oh I thought because you had found the envelope you'd work it out."

I waited. Abbey Road, Beatles titles, got it. My headache came and went in a second.

Michelle on the Rubber Soul album. Eleanor Rigby from Revolver. I responded. *"So you are not about killing, you are trying jihad of the soul."*

"Correct. So we move on. I need an email address. One that is not your work. Can I assume your name at a gmail account?"

I had such an address, it was private of course.

"I can get one."

"Don't try and be clever, look in your in-box, you've already received it."

I look down at my phone, saw he was right and sighed. Of course it wasn't rocket science, who didn't have a gmail account that was just their name? But even so, it was audacious. Why do that, why not just text? Unless it was future proofing for correspondence? Probably? I wanted my thoughts to calm down, instead I had the semblance of a headache emerging just above my right temple.

The email pinged through.

*"**Latitude:** 50° 21' 25.79" N*

***Longitude:** -4° 44' 24.59" W"*

To be honest Geography wasn't my strong point so it could have been anywhere on the planet. I didn't want to be cliched but this really was the stuff of Hollywood, which didn't make sense. This man didn't do the grandiose. He did simple. Trying to compute, to understand, to avoid a trap and yet what trap? Was his modus operandi changing? Was this now the danger? His final text.

"You can bring whoever you like, I won't be there, but I need you to go there nevertheless. Stop and check your emails 10 miles out. Now, this is the first one, the easy one. This is chapter one. Just you and me. A specific discussion, theological I would hope, with reference to a specific place. Remember this is Chapter One. I wish you all the luck in the world."

Having not touched my phone for thirty seconds, it went to sleep.

I paused. My heart was discernibly beating faster, adrenalin was kicking in. I could feel my chest pounding, my head pulsating and getting louder …… louder. I left my desk, passed my phone to someone who tapped in the ordinance reference.

"Eden Project." A disembodied voice, Wilson's I think.

Broughton stared blankly like someone faced with a crossword not knowing where to start.

"Creation," I stated. "This is going to be a theological discussion on creation."

My mind was already racing. I didn't know whether I needed my dad's books or not but I wanted them as a comfort blanket. And I didn't have far to travel to collect them. Our family home, left empty for a year, was in Trethurgy, one mile from the Eden project. For the first time since… I was to go home.

The A303 is a wonderful road to use to the south west if you are tired. The M4 and M5 is mind numbingly boring. Many a head can be seen during the eventide rush hour, bobbing up and down trying to stay awake. The A303 sweeping past Wiltshire towns and villages. The journey down also has a chance of spotting Stonehenge on the right. Testament to the engineering skills of early humanity. How far have we progressed? Great Zimbabwe had the cure for sheep scab a thousand years before the European colonisation of South Africa took the cure north. Mindless violence and greed had not changed, just the means to inflict pain was swifter and more widespread. Each new generation devising ways to eradicate themselves. History has the ability to teach us to avoid the mistakes of the past. Cyclically we return to the same mistakes, generation after generation. The detail may change, the situations remain the same. The virus called humanity is eating at the world from the inside. All it needs is a few rogue cells to turn and fight the virus to save the planet. Was Dalaman Dan a rogue cell? Was he a lunatic? What was he, who was he? Someone flashed and hooted vehemently. I realised I had blinded them with full beam. I needed to concentrate. The sound of an email pinged through from the boot. Exeter services and the final leg home was only a few minutes away. I needed a break anyway so as I joined the M5 for the brief run in to the Granada services I started to dream of a mocha and danish.

I pulled up my Volvo v40 into a car parking space facing the exit. No other car in front. I was two spaces from the edge of the car park so it would be really unlucky if someone hit the car whilst driving past. I pressed the ignition button to switch off the engine as I reached for my bag. I stepped out of the car and a blast of cold winter air hit hard. This was to be quick: toilet, Costa, out.

I paid by card, waited for the mocha, salivated at the danish. As I turned around, the air lodged in my throat, my lips went white, and I felt my face flush. There he was sitting just off to the left by the window and an outside door. He was staring, no he wasn't, he was looking, beckoning for me to join him.

I couldn't quite believe it. My face must have given my shock away but he just smiled. I was too tired to grasp all the possibilities so I simply sat down opposite him and joined him.

As if he read my thoughts he said, "You have a distinctive number plate Miss Ysella, Y55LLA. I passed you just before Stonehenge and just sat a little in front. I must say you caught me a little bit by surprise not signalling to come off here but I was half considering it myself so no damage done." He raised a smile and the coffee.

"So tell me, if you believe in God and the prophet Jesus why doesn't he come back and cure the sick of today. How does he equate all the innocents who suffer in Syria, Afghanistan, the homeless in London, the starving in Haiti. Where is your Jesus then, what does he tell you? Where is Jesus' sign that he is here?"

"Mr Baydar, have you read Shusaku Endo?"

"No."

"He is a Japanese novelist whom my father recommended to all he came across. He wrote novels mainly but he wrote a book on, and called, "The Life of Jesus." He did not try to answer the issue of theodicy therefore I cannot. Like the book of Job my answer can only be, and I quote Bernard-Shaw, "Can you make a Hippopotamus?""

His head rolled back as he laughed. "No I can't."

"Well if you cannot understand how to make a Hippopotamus, then how can I possibly explain why innocent people suffer?" I smiled, a small victory. "But let me send you one of my dad's sermons on Endo. I could email it but if you give me a forwarding address I can post it, save you wasting your ink and paper."

He laughed again.

"I'm not that tired, Miss Ysella. Why don't you tell me what you can remember, my coffee is hot, we've both got time."

I sat there. This was out of my league but my dad had always said that faith should be natural, not forced. There should be a resonance to life, conscience, head and heart.

"My dad loved the Sermon on the Mount. For him, as for Endo, it was a great discourse on love. The scribes, teachers, priests, not even John the Baptist had given a discourse on love such as this. Love was not unknown in the scriptures but none of the prophets had matched this approach by Jesus. His principle of love was directly opposed to the Jewish commentaries regarding the letter of the law. The spirit of forgiveness, of sacrifice, was not something that emanated from the maxims of a successful life. It is a summons to love beyond the abilities of humanity to envisage. This is not what the crowd wanted; here was a response to their nationalistic fervour and it was a total let down. The image of their Messiah was flatly rejected by the man on which they had pinned their hopes. The people were disillusioned. It was their own desire, not Jesus' own portrayal. Did Jesus ever refer to himself as the Messiah? Probably not, but the people wanted signs.

"How different are you, are we? If we do not have tangible, quantifiable results of our faith, the signs and wonders that Jesus lamented we demand, does our faith wane? Blessed are those who believe but have seen no signs or wonders, Jesus said, 'Have you believed because you have seen me? Blessed are those who have not seen and yet have come to believe.'

"There is no hint of God's glory, only the harsh realities of life through which we earnestly and fruitlessly try to discern the genuine love of God. Jesus preached love, a real forgiving sacrificial love but yet grieved life's futility in a world of material values. The hard fact of humanity is we are on the lookout for practical and tangible results. This theme predominates in the Gospels. Jesus said, I think it was in John, but don't quote me……" He smiled an engaging smile that asked me to continue. "'Unless you see signs and wonders, you will not believe.' And when they don't get them, they turn, for as it is written 'those in the Synagogue were filled with rage when they heard him.'

"Now, mostly, love is actually powerless. Love has in itself no immediate tangible benefits. In fact it is often costly, it hurts, it creates tears and heartache. We are therefore hard put to find where the love of

God can be, hidden behind tangible realities which rather suggest that God does not exist, or that he never speaks, or that he is angry. How else do we cope with prayers that seem unanswered, when we pray for answers? Because although one may seemingly be answered here and there, for all the millions of prayers that are prayed each day throughout the world, very few are ever answered as we would wish, and most ultimately will fail or be reversed. Jesus, at the beginning of his ministry, soon realised that what was wanted of him was utilitarian benefits. We will follow you if, we will believe in you if.... but he continued to preach the love of God and the God of love but those who wanted to hear his true meaning were perilously few. His disciples didn't get it, instead they talked amongst themselves about who was to sit on his right, the power, the authority. The disciples were exactly like the other hearers who came to the foothills and shores of Galilee, and why wouldn't they be? They came seeking worldly profit, a break from the harsh realities of their daily lives, not love; costly, sacrificial love. Jesus continually lamented that they all asked for a sign.

"And that is the the problem once more with our faith today, you asked for a sign and in reality don't we all? The disciples were pretty much like the rest of us, a collection of no good cowards and weaklings who didn't get it. And we are no different. We look for utilitarian profit, in whatever way we see it, for ourselves. We want to feel love, but somehow we want to see it for ourselves, that we are loved and perhaps they over there are not. We are the chosen people, therefore they over there are not. We haven't changed. It is part of our humanity. Jesus saw this and loved us and died for the weakling and the coward that are us, and our faith is called to respond. Not that we love God, but that God loves us. We don't believe because we have seen the love of God. 'Blessed are those,' says Jesus, 'who believe and yet have not seen'. That is faith. It is easy to believe when you have seen the miracles and yet what about those stories of Jesus which are different.

"The Gospels have many stories about Jesus and the lost and rejected. There are, according to Endo, two kinds. The first, the miracle healing stories and the other consolation stories where Jesus simply shares with them in their pitiable sufferings. For me the consolation stories have a greater sense of reality. They demonstrate more the character of Jesus, the real Jesus. Like the sinful woman who when she knew where he was took to him an alabaster jar of ointment, bathed his feet with kisses and dried them with his hair. Now the Pharisee said to himself, 'If this man were a prophet, he would have known who and what kind of woman this is.' Jesus told him this parable: 'A certain creditor had two debtors. One owed five hundred denarii, and the other fifty. When they could not pay, he cancelled the debts for both of them. Now, which of them will love him more?' The Pharisee answered 'I suppose the one for whom he cancelled the greater debt.' And Jesus said to him, 'You are right. This woman has done so much for me this evening and you have not. Therefore, I tell you, her sins, which were many, have been forgiven, hence she has shown great love. But the one to whom little is forgiven, loves little.'"

He smiled. "I know the story, and I suppose the haemorrhaging woman from St Mark's Gospel makes the same point."

I must have looked surprised.

"Miss Ysella, I have had many months to read and think about the world. Whether I believe in it or not, Christianity is a major force of power and control in the world."

"So then," I continued, "you see it is not about the healing. What is the wonderment is that Jesus felt all the woman's heartbreak and suffering through the touch of her finger against his clothing. In the consolation stories, which need no explanation, which aren't tinged with a sort of magic, but yet express clearly the life like picture of Jesus, Jesus is spending time on these sorrows in the sort of men and women to whom others paid no attention at all. For Jesus knew that poverty and disease are not necessarily the hardest things to bear, the hardest thing is to live in the loneliness and hopelessness that accompanies disease and poverty. It is that which he sought to overcome and that which we can also do."

At last he responded. "There you go, we agree. Religion is for signs, but it doesn't work. Let us get rid of this religion and live in reality. Look at it simply; suicide bombings in Kabul, how many killed in Mindanao?"

"But religion is about living in reality, or at least it should be. What I am saying is that religion is getting it wrong again, but that doesn't mean it is wrong."

I sat back and sighed. Now I was exhausted.

"Could you email me any of those sermons you think I would like?"

I looked blankly.

He suddenly looked uncomfortable as if he had overstepped the mark. I suddenly realised that here was a man who was a student of life. Maybe I could change this pattern of events after all. He was talking, shuffling to get up.

"Now I must go. I've got a few things to do in the morning. Get some rest, little one."

I shuddered as if someone had walked over my grave. My Dad used to call me 'little one.' He disappeared into the night through the side door. I should have gone after him, I should have arrested him but something in me wanted to defeat him at his own game. He had a face that was indistinguishable yet memorable. Perhaps it was the kindness that came from him. He truly believed in his ideology which now, the more I thought, was reminiscent of the struggles of Endo. As soon as I could understand, my Dad had given me his passion for Endo. I was back at the car and suddenly remembered that I could grab his DNA from the cup. I span round straight into an elderly couple making their way to their car. I mumbled an apology and ran back to Costa.

The waitress had cleared the table and I half barked, "The cups from that table, where are they?"

She pointed to the trays stacked high on a trolley. I examined and look at them and decided on one that had no lipstick. I couldn't be sure. I flashed my warrant card and exited for a second time.

♦

Damir sat in his car and watched the girl run back to the cafe area and return with a cup in her hand.

"Damn." He had been silly to meet with her face to face, but he longed for some human contact and he felt drawn to this girl. The few minutes they spent together gave him a joy of life. He had his mission that he needed to fulfil. That was his duty to his father who had saved him. A mission to save the world from itself by uniting against misguided religions of all persuasion. But in those few moments he felt the sheer exuberance of life. But now she had his DNA. It shouldn't matter, he was who he was, but still he had an uncomfortable feeling about it. With a flick of his head and turn of the ignition key he dismissed the thought from his mind. The Volvo V40 had left the car park already and he was in no mind to catch it again. So instead of taking the slip road into the A30 five minutes later he travelled straight down the A38 and entered Cornwall across the Tamar bridge.

♦

"Sir, I need a DNA check on a mug."

"Whose?"

There was a pause. A sigh. A mumbled, "I'm not going to like this am I?" The air of resignation enfolded Broughton.

"No sir, you're not."

"Please spare me the details. Just take it to the nearest police station and give them my number, I'll sort out the rest."

I had pulled up on the drive of the home I hadn't seen for a year. I opened the wooden gates. I let the car crawl over the gravel. The overhead lights from the garage came on with the motion. Using the torch on my phone I illuminated the key safe box and turned the dials to find the numbers. I opened the door, replaced the key in its box and as I entered the alarm sounded. I deftly keyed in the number and all was silence. I turned on the hall light though we didn't really have a hall. The Moroccan style tiles beneath my feet gave way to off white tiles covering the vast expanse of the predominantly open plan downstairs. I trudged up the stairs. The landing and lounge here were also open planned. I dumped my bag in my room, a room that I had had from childhood and walked to the woodburner and ten minutes later could feel the warmth from the fire thawing out the room. Downstairs there was a small wine cabinet and there, as there always had been, was at least one bottle of Rioja. I opened it, let it breath as I got into my pyjamas.

My parents' office was just off the kitchen and it was there I found myself, glass in hand, perusing their book shelves. I picked up a book, "The Groaning of Creation". My dad hadn't read it, you could tell, it was still in good condition. I put it down on the chaise longue and carried on looking. Several books by Endo, first edition; immaculate, and other copies thumbed and well worn. I found Hick, "The Myth of God Incarnate" and next to it my father's notebooks. He had a thousand ideas a second and more often than not he couldn't keep up with them so he jotted them down in several black notebooks. Hick, Southgate and the notebooks accompanied me up to the lounge, with the rest of the bottle cradled between arm and body.

Hick had his time before my dad was ordained. He and Geoffrey Lampe had an extraordinary impact on a young man who could have easily played the part of a vicar and trotted out the same banal rubbish. Instead he wrestled and wrestled as he tried to give expression to what he called a real faith. Of course this did not make him necessarily popular with those in the 'club', but to those who stood on the periphery looking in, Dad's honest take on his own struggles appealed. He was the centurion who said, "Lord, I believe. Help my unbelief." Dad took seriously the arguments against the existence of God and believed that Christianity needed to fight on a new battleground. Like everyone before him he wanted the words of Jesus to make sense in a new generation. The Church, though paying lip service to such an approach, is at its core traditional. My dad, as so many of his colleagues had, lamented to his tired congregation that actually the Church was more pharisaical than the Pharisees two thousand years before. They left the service, shook his hand at the door saying, "Nice service Vicar", not really having grasped the full meaning of what he was trying to say. Of course when they did grasp the full meaning when he had, in his words, 'got it right', there were mutterings of discontent.

I could sense that, metaphorically, Damir Baydar looked in from the outside. He saw the need to change and it was obvious he was engaged. This wasn't a zealot, this was a man who saw better for the world. So just what was it that had made him take the decision to inflict terror? This wasn't a power crazed junkie. He wasn't so many things. So what was he?

I leafed through the notebooks and found my glass perilously lolling over. Time for bed. Who knows what the morning will bring. I texted my mum.

"I'm here. Home. Hope you're ok?"

A heart and a thumbs up came immediately back. "Good night mumma, good night dadda," I whispered.

Chapter Seven- Creation

I checked my emails as I had originally been asked. Of course I wasn't ten miles out, only one. He wasn't to know that.

It had been sent an hour before as a PDF attachment. Black coffee and paracetamol in hand, I snuggled on one of the downstairs sofas and read.

The tabloids have nicknamed me Dalaman Dan. I am Damir Baydar but you want to know who I am, my motivation? Who I am now is not who I was. To be honest I don't know who I was, what I was like, what I did. Some pretty unsavoury things I would guess, for I have a deep seated guilt wallowing somewhere in my soul. I have been given a new chance by my father to make a difference in the world, to give the world a fighting chance for survival. This kind of resurrection has given me a lot of affinity with the stories of Jesus before it got tainted by the parasites of the Church. I've googled your name. I see your father was a Priest. I am truly sorry for the circumstances surrounding his death. He and I would have been contemporaries for his last year at Cambridge but our paths would not have crossed. I was not into religion in any way then. Over the last year I have studied hard. The Jesus stories fascinate me. I think Jesus was torn between the martyr's death he ultimately chose and a revolution. It was a genuine struggle for him and because of that his disciples themselves got confused with many indeed believing he was a revolutionary. It was the fourth temptation before the last temptation as identified by Kazantsakis. Of course Kasantsakis saw Jesus as human and divine whereas for me the human Jesus resonates far better. I can understand this more, rather than putting this divinity in a veil of flesh.

Unless of course we are all divinity in a veil of flesh, that the incarnation is not a single moment. That is a whole different matter, a totally different concept and one I fear we may never have the time to discuss.

Do you remember when Jesus enters into a Samaritan village where he isn't welcomed, the disciples are incredulous and Jesus refuses to let the disciples turn the situation into a 'them and us' scenario. Humanity is very good at turning all situations into 'us and them.' The only time people unite is against a common enemy. I am that enemy for your sakes.

Jesus says don't identify yourselves as being separate to others- don't take a stand where you identify yourselves as not them. We identify ourselves as not being like others rather than actually identifying ourselves as us and what we are. Most British have genetics and DNA that relate to Angles, Saxons, Vikings, Romans- most of your ancestors are European. Ironic, yes? There are very few pure Celtic genealogies left in England.

People spend so much of their lives trying to compartmentalise themselves in relation with others and it simply doesn't work. We evolve, develop, mature, regress. Heightened stresses in lives mean so many revert back to being a person they thought they had laid to rest many years before. We can't look back, we can't look forward we can only live in the moment. One of Immanuel Kant's elements of the categorical imperative is that when one makes a moral decision one cannot think about what impact it may have in the future, one can only reason whether it is the right moral thing to do now.

That actually provides the security of the moment. The Samaritan village felt insecure because they were seeing Jesus set on going to Jerusalem. What trouble would he cause there? Would he throw over tables in the temple? Would people draw their swords in the garden of Gethsemane? How would the authorities treat his obvious popularity and what would the comeback be on the Samaritan village if it all went wrong? Would there be genocide from Herod as retribution for aiding and abetting this itinerant prophet? So their response: "Nope, we don't want him."

And then Jesus, as they continued on their journey, started to talk. People were saying how much they were going to do, and Jesus, possibly having heard it all before, turned on them and made them realise the folly of their words because he was set toward Jerusalem and he essentially knew the future before him. He attacked the emptiness of their promises, the foolishness, because they didn't understand what they were saying. They were committing themselves to a future that they couldn't control, were identifying themselves with a future they didn't understand. They were craving an identity that would give them stability and security. A very human thing to do. How do we feel safe and secure, what grouping do we identify ourselves with? Identity is often determined by where we live. I'm Turkish, I'm Syrian, I'm English. Jesus is pointing out that actually to be his follower isn't about having an identity, not an identity based on a home not even an identity as being a disciple of Christ, because that turns identity into us and them again, but actually we can only live in the moment. We can't live in the past, as he points out to the disciple who wants to bury his father, he says let the dead bury the dead.

Now let me tell you a story.

A guy named Bob receives a free ticket to the European Cup final from his company. Unfortunately, when Bob arrives at the stadium he realises the seat is in the last row in the corner of the stadium - he's closer to the Goodyear blimp than the field.

About halfway through the first half, Bob notices an empty seat 10 rows off the field, right on the half way line. He decides to take a chance and makes his way through the stadium and around the security guards to the empty seat. As he sits down, he asks the gentleman sitting next to him, "Excuse me, is anyone sitting here?" The man says no.

Now, very excited to be in such a great seat for the game, Bob again inquires of the man next to him, "This is incredible! Who in their right mind would have a seat like this at the European Cup final and not use it?"

The man replies, "Well, actually, the seat belongs to me, I was supposed to come with my wife, but she passed away. This is the first cup final we haven't been together at since we got married in 1967 the year that Celtic won."

"Well, that's really sad," says Bob, "but still, couldn't you find someone to take the seat? A relative or close friend?"

"No," the man replies, "they're all at the funeral."

I'm sorry if it is too close to the bone, but it is a good story making a good point. I understand. I believe my father who so nursed me for the last year, taught me everything I now know, is dead. I haven't returned, I have stayed to complete the task he entrusted to me. A task to save the world from itself. I understand a little of your pain. The point though is well made. Jesus says it one way, this joke says it another; let go of the past, we can't limit our identity to the past, we have to, as the gentleman did in the joke, live in the present that has been built on the past. He honoured his wife's memory more by doing in the present what she would have done should she have been with him.

But we can't live just in the future either. We can't think to ourselves I could change my future if this happened or that happened; so another story-

A man walking along a beach deep in prayer. All of a sudden he said out loud, "Lord grant me one wish."

Suddenly the sky clouded above his head and in a booming voice the Lord said, "Because you have been faithful to me in all ways, I will grant you one wish."

The man said, "Build a bridge to Canada so I can drive over anytime I want to."

The Lord said, "Your request is very materialistic. Think of the logistics of that kind of undertaking. The supports required to reach the bottom of the Atlantic! The concrete and steel it would take! I can do it, but it is hard for me to justify your desire for worldly things. Take a little more time and think of another wish, a wish you think would honour and glorify me."

The man thought about it for a long time. Finally he said, "Lord, I have had many relationships in my life and all my partners and daughters said that I am uncaring and insensitive. I wish that I could understand women. I want to know how they feel inside, what they are thinking when they give me the silent treatment, why they cry, what they mean when they say "nothing" and how I can make a woman truly happy."

After a few minutes God said, "You want two lanes or four on that bridge?"

I love it. I think in my past there were always women around me. Sisters I know of, my mother. They all died at the same time, but I think friends too. I don't know if I had daughters but I hope they would grow to be as tenacious and thoughtful as you.

Back to my point. We need to ask ourselves, how do we identify ourselves? We cannot identify ourselves as them and us, that doesn't reflect who we are, merely who we don't want to be- which is unhealthy, unrealistic. To identify ourselves with the past can give a false identity to who we are and who others are. After all, remember I have no past that I understand. We cannot always judge from the past either.

Live in the moment. Live who you are now, it may feel insecure and unstable but it doesn't have to feel that way. We cannot identify ourselves and form ourselves by that which is outside of ourselves. We are created by God for who we are, so right at this moment like yourself for who you are, that is the only identity we truly have.

Now let the games begin :) DD.

I sat there. So much to take in. Were there clues in here that could help stop this man? My job of course was simply to catch him and I had had my chance last night. Something though told me that I needed to defeat his philosophical argument. The problem was philosophically I agreed, and I know my dad would have agreed with everything. Everything except the method of changing people's perceptions. Although, Dad had his moments of extremism as he furrowed his brow and rubbed his temples. Predominantly these were moments of trying to work out how the Church would pay all of its bills.

For the first time visitor, the Eden Project is an amazing experience. The Biomes, Mediterranean and Tropical, house such a variety of plants that suddenly humanity appears quite insignificant. Until of course you discover as you journey through not only how humanity is destroying the environment but also how it easy it would be for humanity to repair it. The realm of politics then enters the sphere and good people are turned off.

Every need for each family is catered for with the obligatory shop and cafe areas. It is almost always full. As a family, my parents would take me down there for a bowl of soup. I would bolt down half the soup and then watch the spectacle in the entrance hall of the wooden mannequins in their home go up and down as the story of our dependence on nature was told. It is amazing how small moments can make such an impact.

I wound myself down the hairpin bends of a footpath that takes you to, amongst other attractions, the Biomes. The great event shed was preparing for the winter ice rink that I remember my friends and I using during the Christmas holiday.

Back to the present. Baydar. I wasn't sure what the game was but I did know I had already lost. The fact I was here, early in the morning with only the first few visitors for company meant I was already too late. The bomb, if you could call it that, would already be in situ. Perhaps for days. Although maybe not? After all, he was in Exeter. Broughton had wanted Eden closed to visitors so the bomb could be found and deactivated without problem. I had argued against. None of the bombs had hurt anyone. They were designed to create terror, to demonstrate that everyone was vulnerable. To provoke fear and I guess a change of direction.

A text message blipped through. It was Broughton. *"Come over to the Bridge that connects to 'The Seed'."*

I saw him standing in the distance on the bridge above.

I started to walk over. It took a few minutes and I was stood beside him. He hadn't moved an inch.

"What are we thinking?"

"Sir, you're here?"

"Early flight. Didn't like the fact he was able to engage with you last night. I pushed through forensics. Sorry to tell you, you picked up the wrong cup and it was dirty. Makes you think about just exactly what you are putting in your mouth these days." He flicked a hand away to stop any response. "Anyway, it was your cup, basically your DNA. Red herring anyway. What did you expect to find? We know who he is."

"I don't know sir, just something…." I tailed off. It was a ridiculous chase but then Broughton was also inquisitive.

An email pinged through on my phone.

"Did God create the world or did science create the world?"

"What?" Broughton on my shoulder was exasperated.

"Go with it sir."

"But are you supposed to get the right answer to prevent the explosion?"

"Sir, I don't know."

"So what it is then?"

"Well, science explains the process of how the world was created, but the question lies behind, was it deliberate or was it a cosmic accident? If deliberate then it could be attributed to something that we call God. The creation narratives in Genesis give an explanation as to the why of creation, not the how. Yet if creation is an accident, what are the chances of that? Are you a gambler sir?" He frowned. "It is down to probabilities."

"Yes yes I get that" he pouted. "So what is the answer he wants?"

"I don't know sir, but I will give the answer he thinks." I typed.

"We don't know what, if anything, created the world but science gives us more understanding of how it was created. And not in seven days as we understand seven days."

We waited. Ping.

"Good. Does creation continue to happen? Is it more an evolutionary process? Or a one off event?"

"Ongoing, evolutionary." I typed back and pressed send. Ping.

"Good. So are we a part of this creation?"

"Yes" Ping.

"Good. Are we destroying it, the Amazon forest, the ozone layer, the natural minerals, the ice caps. Are we destroying that which we are a part of creating?"

I hesitated. *"Tes"* I hit the wrong key but it didn't matter, I pressed send anyway. Ping.

"Are people responding to the campaigns pointing out to them the perils of what they are doing?"

I hesitated. I could see where this was leading.

"Yes" Send. Ping.

"But would they respond to say a shock that would be clearly demonstrate this error. The ice cap slowly melts and no one gives a damn. But if a flood took out London, then what?"

The enormity was hitting.

I typed, *"They would take notice."* I pressed send, and at that moment in the building to our right, as we surveyed the rest of the Eden Project, there was an explosion. In that moment I realised what had happened. The building was intact and mercifully the doors to it were still locked for maintenance. It was too early for maintenance so it was empty. So when the 'SEED' came crashing down through the building destroying it internally there were no casualties. The Press were going to have a field day. Tomorrow's headlines would be derivatives of "Dalaman Dan destroys Seed of Hope". Not that we would confirm it immediately but to keep the panic at bay we would, eventually by the end of the day, have to. A philosophical journey of going back and forth, or was it round and round, was about to begin. An argument with a man arguing with himself I felt. This was 'The Shack' meets 'Jason Bourne'. Dad didn't like 'The Shack' but he liked the original Bourne books by Ludlum. Suddenly a thought came to my mind. *"Was that it?"* I typed. *"No theological discussion about creation? Some game!"* was my final sarcastic comment. I was hurting as if I had been abused. I wanted to wrestle in hand to hand theological combat. Ping.

"Each game will be different."

"It isn't a game!" Send.

I couldn't quite believe that I had so quickly become so impassioned. The "Seed" was a symbol of my childhood. My dad running round and round after me, or so I thought. He had actually just stood at the entrance drinking his coffee and making growling sounds each time I approached so I would run back the other way. The game of endless excitement to me always lasted just long enough for him to drink his extra large mocha. That was why I was angry, because anger it was. Ping.

"It is, mind against mind, heart against heart and no one will get hurt, until the final game. You will win."

"?" Send. Ping.

"Love"

Chapter Eight- Love

As Broughton flew back to London, I drove. I looked at every driver I passed. And I passed many. I had insisted on driving so Broughton had ensured a police escort. I was at Millbank in two and a half hours. I briefed Wilson and Jenkins more with the facts than with what I surmised. Broughton had told me to keep it brief leaving out the meeting at Exeter Services.

Broughton was struggling with the furore in the press and yet the lack of deaths. It was terrorism. It needed to be stopped. But it was like he was a gentlemen terrorist. The Scarlet Pimpernel, Nelson Mandela, Robin Hood, any genuine hero you could think of that kicked against the Establishment. I represented the Establishment. Dad was proud of my achievements but the Establishment always bristled with him. I often joked that there was nothing less Establishment than the Church of England, and he would smile, tussle my hair and caress the argument with "Change from within. Put a frog into boiling water, it will leap out. Put a frog into cold water and gently heat the water and you have your supper." He purred with delight when he felt he was on the winning side of an argument. In a household of predominantly women this was a rare occasion.

A grey suited indistinguishable man appeared at the door and we all looked up. Grantham, the studious member of the team who didn't talk much, but didn't need to, took the envelope from him, glanced at the name and passed the envelope to Broughton who absent-mindedly opened it.

"Well, some semblance of good news at last." He passed the note to me.

I breathed a huge sigh of relief as I read that the Turkish authorities had released Ruby Greene without charge, apologising for any misunderstandings and that she was already on a plane to London. Turkey's richest man, Maaravi Uysal, a food magnate, was looking to invest in the U.K., rumour had it at a football club, but then rumour had it that Brexit would be a good deal for Britain. Uysal had become friends with one Neal Greene. Uysal had brokered the deal, it was pretty obvious that Turkey wanted to distance itself from Baydar and was giving an olive branch to demonstrate international cooperation etc etc etc. I gave the letter back to Broughton who passed it on to Grantham. "You two," he looked at Grantham and Jenkins who were standing next to each other, "meet Miss Greene at Heathrow…." I tried to cut him off. "She's flying from Istanbul," Broughton ventured, by way of answering my unasked question without actually acknowledging me at all. He continued deliberately towards Jenkins and Grantham. "Bring her back. Chat with her. Make sure she is all right. Debrief her but I don't expect the report to be any longer than a page. The poor girl needs to get back to her family as soon as possible. Take her wherever she wants." The two departed, grabbing jackets as they left. "You," said Broughton, directing his attention to me. Go home, go for a run, read a book or do whatever you do to relax." I left.

I arrived at my one and a half bedroomed Shepherd's Bush flat which was on the first floor above a Tesco Express. I queued at the checkout for some croissants, made a coffee upstairs, ate the croissants and fell asleep on the sofa. While I slept, Grantham and Jenkins returned to Millbank with Ruby Greene.

♦

"Is everything all right?" Broughton rose from his chair as the three of them entered the office. "Ms Greene, How are you? I'm so glad you are safe. I've asked my men to take you home. Is everything ok?" His words were tripping out of his mouth as he had taken an amphetamine. He was enamoured of the wealthy and powerful and behaved like a serf fighting for his life around them. Ruby smiled, an ingratiating smile.

"Sir," Grantham answered. "There is something you must know." He handed the Times daily over to Broughton. On the front page was a picture of Damir Baydar, aka Dalaman Dan.

"I've seen him before." Simple, to the point, Ruby was never known to mince her words.

Broughton didn't flinch. He was working through all the facts, the timings. Ruby Greene had not been in the U.K when the bombings had started.

"Coffee?" he asked.

"Tea," was the flat reply. Ruby Greene could be the sweetest most adoring of women with her demure smile. Those moments tended to be around animals. With authoritarian figures of which Broughton was certainly one she was monosyllabic, tentative and cautious verging on distrustful with a tendency to appear rude. "I'm not rude," she would yell at her sisters during their teenage years. "You are just annoying me." Not a lot had changed except now she spent almost all of her time with animals so she rarely got annoyed. At least that was how she saw it.

She picked up the paper and threw it across Broughton's desk. The front side up.

"I've seen him before. The night before I got kidnapped." The 'kidnapped' was pointed, her nose moving towards his face, her face expressive in its displeasure. "He was the waiter at the Olive Garden." She noted Broughton's face crease with a question forming. "A restaurant in Kabak just outside of Oludeniz. It has a pool, chalets, nice place to go to spend an afternoon. My sisters and I went there and he was the waiter who served us. He spoke English, French and Russian apparently."

The 'apparently' was off hand, thinking of her sisters' love-life was something she had never wished to dwell on. As if sensing Broughton's next question bluntly she reported that that was all she knew. Broughton, taken aback and certainly not used to being spoken to in that way, at least not at work, stuttered, "I think, I think though, I think though it may be, it is, we should actually, if it is all right, well we need to speak to your," he glanced down at a piece of paper that wasn't there, and then guessed, "your two sisters?"

The Ruby pout appeared.

Broughton found the pout endearing. "Well anyway, we need to speak to them."

Ruby frowned. Millbank was intimidating.

"Are they close?"

"Well they were going to meet me off the plane. We were going to spend a night in London and then go to our mother's. They are in London." She glanced at her phone. "Hayward Gallery."

"Excellent. Shall we all grab a coffee………" Broughton was cut short by Ruby's frown.

"Tea," he continued. "Hayward Gallery it is."

It is only just over a mile from Thames House Millbank to the Hayward Gallery. They walked across Lambeth Bridge and started eastwards along the Albert Embankment. They were passing St Thomas' hospital when the sound of a text message on Ruby's phone brought a change of plan. "Ned's noodle bar," she said. "They've moved," she offered by way of explanation.

"Excellent," said Broughton. It was nearer.

Broughton, Grantham and Jenkins found the three Greene girls captivating. They were everything they were purported to be. Intelligent, strong willed, beautiful. Grantham and Sapphire talked easily one to another as if they were old friends. Ruby took advantage of the opportunity of fading out of the limelight. Filippa spoke to Broughton. Decisive, factual. Jenkins made copious notes. Eventually after a long discussion that inevitably turned into lunch, Broughton stood up and thanked the Greene girls for their assistance. They had a flight to catch. The girls left, smiles all round. The waiter appeared. Broughton looked aghast. Filippa Greene for one earned more in a day than he did in a year and he was picking up the tab. The alcohol bill made his eyes water. They had discerning taste these Greene girls, discerning taste.

As they walked inland from the Thames, Filippa winked at her sisters, they exchanged high fives. "Result," she said. To those who have, more will be given.

By the end of day Grantham and Jenkins found themselves on a plane out of Gatwick heading towards the Olive Garden at Kabak.

♦

When I awoke I was a little disorientated. My head pounding felt like I had lived a whole life in one day. Perhaps I had. Love. Love. Love! What was going to happen? Actually I knew what would happen- a small explosion. The question was, where? Love? Valentine? Nope, love is love? God is love. God is love and…….. God is love and those who live in love live in God and God lives in them. The opening sentence of the Church of England marriage service. As a baby when my mum was working I had conducted many marriages in the arms of my father. As a toddler I would sit on the front row with a bridesmaid and as a child I would sit in the creche area before progressing to his computer in the Church office. I was always there, listening and obviously taking it all in. So marriage: is it related to faith? Anything to do with faith at all? What would that discussion be? I picked up the phone and rang Broughton. Before I could speak, I heard his voice.

"We have a lead. Here, you have an hour." The phone went dead.

I arrived not to a frenzy of activity that I expected but to an almost empty office. "They've gone to Turkey. Ruby Greene only had her dinner served by Baydar the night before she was taken. I've sent Tweedle Dee and Dum over to see if they can glean anything." Broughton was on edge as if he had missed something. "What about you? Got any leads on love?"

"Yes," I began.

"I want the synopsis."

"Oh," my deflated response. "Okay. Ummmm. Where does one go to get married?"

"Is that it? Is that all you can come up with on love? Marriage?"

"No sir. It is more to do with his starting point of God. In the marriage service the opening sentence." His eyes were glazing over.

"Anyway it comes down to where does one go to get married?"

"Registry office, Church, that narrows down the possibilities with three of us here!" Broughton was losing his cool.

"Gretna Green," Wilson's voice in the corner spoke up. He looked at us and said it again. "Gretna Green, symbolic with marriage, and more particularly love. Those who loved but for whom marriage in their local Church was not an option. So they married for true love in the place where they could."

"Genius." Broughton was impressed.

Why hadn't I thought of that. Oh well it didn't matter.

Wilson stayed in London. Broughton and I caught the plane to Edinburgh and hired a car to Gretna Green. As he drove out of the city my phone pinged an email.

"Jesus came to bring love in a common sense approach to communal living. He was not trying to proselytise for members of the club, but simply trying to enable everyone to live, truly live. Jesus wasn't about setting up another religion. For Mark and Luke the story is trying to tell us that the two Kingdoms, the Jesus Kingdom and the world kingdom can be reconciled, that there are people on both sides who recognise and agree in the validity of the other. That is what we need. Not furthering the power of the few at the expense of the many.

So what can this mean for the world?- how do we live out the commandment that if we love Jesus we will fulfil his commandments? Christians must in the name of Jesus lay down their doctrines, do a unilateral disarmament of doctrine that will truly love, enemy included. Then they will recognise the validity of the position of those who may not live in our realm but where the two kingdoms agree we will acknowledge the righteousness of the other side. That the commandments are there as broad life-living principles. What does this mean?

Well, it alludes to the futility of nationalism, to the pointlessness of having a "them and us" dialogue. We are one global world and yet we continuously want to break it down into small constituent parts. That is because in all our thinking we spend our time thinking and praying about what is right for us. This is simply wrong. To be a Christian is to think about what is right for others and this is no academic exercise that has limited relevancy in our daily lives. How do you vote? Will you now vote to suit your desires or will you vote to support the poor and marginalised, the refugee and the asylum seeker which may cost you more? Do you really follow Jesus' command to love him and to follow his commandments, or do we only do so when it suits us. Do you know there are 613 Jewish commandments. That is why it got summarised into two. There are 248 positive commandments corresponding to the parts of the body and 365 negative commandments corresponding to the days of the year. Do you hear about those. The fact you break at least one Levitical commandment every day in the normal course of living. So the greatest commandment is love. Do you? Answer me this question- does love cost?"

I waited, I let my thoughts find some kind of order in my brain. There were clues here. He was trying to catch me out - Sadducees.

Commandments- therefore Sadducees. But this was about love. Sadducees. Love.

"Got it."

Broughton looked at me blankly.

I typed. *"That story when the Sadducees tried to catch Jesus out on marriage laws."* Send. Ping.

"Well done. Yes they were trying to catch him out using Deuteronomy 25."

I googled the passage and read, 'When brothers reside together, and one of them dies and has no son, the wife of the deceased shall not be married outside the family to a stranger. Her husband's brother shall go in to her, taking her in marriage, and performing the duty of a husband's brother to her, and the firstborn whom she bears shall succeed to the name of the deceased brother, so that his name may not be blotted out of Israel.'

Broughton read it over my shoulder whilst trying to negotiate the closing time traffic.

"What does it mean?" he asked.

"Essentially, in Old Testament times it means if your brother has a heart condition make sure you have a say in who he marries."

He looked at me and raised an eyebrow. He then laughed. A laugh that broke the tension.

"Look," I continued. "Marriage for many centuries was about family honour, about property. It is a tool to enable us to function more effectively."

"You've haven't seen my marriage," he interjected chuckling.

"Judaism teaches that God has a covenant with the whole of humanity that doesn't need the marriage laws. This is all about the children of Israel's identification with land. The covenants with God were land based. Then you throw in Hosea likening God's covenant to a marriage. The covenant theology as it is now termed gave Israel an identity. Identity is something that we know is important to DD. Remember that email before the Eden Project."

I quickly looked it up and quoted, "They were craving an identity that would give them stability and security. A very human thing to do. How do we feel safe and secure, what grouping do we identify ourselves with?"

I paused.

"You know what Jesus did whenever he was asked a question. He answered it with a question. So let us see…." I typed.

"So is the Kingdom of heaven like a marriage?" Send.

I waited only a few moments. We arrived at Gretna Green. To keep us stimulated we got out of the car and observed the iconic window towering above the front door. Ping. Back to reality.

"Jesus pointedly said No! So what did Jesus say it was like?" was the emailed response.

"Damn another question." Broughton, I felt, was out of his depth.

"Relax sir. This isn't rocket science, it is the theological understandings not of a professor but of someone who has read and wrestled and is trying to define his own conclusions knowing that he will probably never conclude them at all."

"No, it is man who is bringing fear to the whole nation. If he can do it, what about the nutty copy cats."

"Sir," I was firm. "If we treat him as a terrorist we won't get to him. We need to treat him as someone who is wrestling with God, like Jacob at Peniel."

"And….?"

"Jacob and God wrestled and both had their lives, according to the story, changed forever. So down to the Kingdom of Heaven. What is the Kingdom of Heaven like?"

I typed;

"The Kingdom of Heaven grows, is something that once you've found it is all that you want. It is full of forgiveness but those who cannot forgive in return aren't welcome. It is all embracing, all encompassing, no rules, no covenants. It

is for all of the love you have ever lived, for love is eternal and that love grows like the mustard seed in the Kingdom of Heaven." Send. Ping.

"That is what Jesus taught. How far away are religions from that and in particular those who call themselves the followers of Christ?"

"A long way away." I typed and pressed send immediately. Ping.

"So do they need to start loving.?"

An immediate, *"Yes"* I typed. Send. Ping.

"So does love cost?"

The adrenalin, which had been mounting, dissipated from my body and I felt like I had grown pale. If I said yes, which was of course the truthful answer, the explosion would happen. If I said 'No', what would happen?

I paused. A message came through, I hadn't heard the ping.

"The answer is of course yes, but will it happen if you say no? Will I unleash unfathomable powers? Of course not. It isn't a game where you have three lives. It is a game where I want you to open your eyes to the needs of the world. If you say No, you throw away your love and your life will have no meaning. You have to say yes because it is the truth Doris."

Broughton looked over my shoulder. "Doris?"

"Doris Day......."

"Che sera, of course, what will be will be. Ok say we know it isn't a test with right and wrong answers. Tell the truth."

I typed- *"YES love costs."* I pressed send and the explosion happened. It caught me unawares. There were no bins outside the registry office at Gretna Green so I wasn't quite sure where the explosion would be. Broughton and I had conspired deliberately to get there in the middle of the night so there would no witnesses and the furore in the press wouldn't get ignited. Dalaman Dan was having an effect on the country, no one felt safe, because ordinary towns, ordinary places were targeted. Not just the big cities.

Months later forensics would explain in great detail the location of the small explosives at just the right points, so the explosion was actually many ones all contriving to bring down the registry office at Gretna Green from the inside. No casualties. No exploding out but an internal combustion. There was no way of keeping this secret. The building was a pile of rubble. Ping.

"Power"

Wilson and I were not expected to go to our respective homes and so, on our return to London, Broughton and I summarised everything we knew including the meeting at Exeter. Wilson raised his eyes in surprise.

Broughton was not used to drawing dead ends. Nothing made sense in a straightforward logical way. He must have been like his predecessors when first confronted with guerrilla warfare. Unbeknown to me he was actually worrying about Baydar becoming a hero. Civil disobedience with an ideological agenda that many would have sympathy with if only they knew. Perhaps they should know. We were going round in circles. Apparently his wife took a lot of persuading that the expensive lunch with the Greene girls would eventually be met in expenses. He had though had a roasting especially as a friend of hers reported that they were all drinking whilst at work. He was not having a good couple of days.

"Who knows a psychologist?" Broughton flung his hands to his temples in exasperation. "I don't want a profiler, I want an expert, and I want that expert now!"

The reverberation of the final word echoed and held all the room.

I broke the silence.

"I do."

"Who?" It seemed more of an accusation than a question.

"Jacintia Greene."

"Who?"

"Mrs Jacintia Greene."

"I know what you said, I am asking who the hell is she and why suddenly is everybody called Greene?"

I pondered my next sentence and decided to be upfront at this level.

"Because it is the same family, Mrs Greene, the Greene girls' Mother is a psychologist. Well respected in her field, used to working with the police."

I was measured, not rushed, I needed an aura of calm.

"Make the call."

"I have her number at home….."

He cut me off. "I don't give a damn where you make the call just make the goddamn call."

I grabbed my bag and left the office. I took the underground to Shepherd's Bush. I was just like any traveller, except the tourists. I was face down in a book, not attracting any attention to myself. Once in my flat, I picked up the phone. I didn't need to look at the number, it was pre-programmed into my mobile. It rang, the dial tone signalling it was an international call. The tone stopped ringing and a familiar voice answered.

"Mum, I really need a favour."

Chapter Nine- Power

Filling your mother in on what was happening in your life at the same time as your sisters are filling her in on what was happening in theirs is not easy, nigh on impossible. They were face to face and included a kidnapping. I was losing out in the battle of the conversations. Eventually she must have taken the phone to another room.

"Do you want me to fly over tomorrow?" she asked.

"Please Mum."

"Okay. Get some sleep. Take a melatonin if you need to."

Jacintia Greene was brought from Heathrow. She now sat at Thames House being told absolutely everything. She made notes on a pad that I had got for her. Doodles and arrows.

"Well?" Broughton asked eventually.

"Personality disorder obviously. But how did that disorder develop? From birth? Childhood? Was it some kind of trauma? Or was it something else? Hypnotherapy can be discounted because it is a trait change not a state change. This is a state change. He said resurrection and talked of amnesia, yes?"

"He referred to it without mentioning it specifically," Broughton offered. I was keeping quiet.

"What is the next target?"

"We don't know, but the subject is power."

"Divisive," she retorted.

"Psychotic!"

"No sir." Mum was firm and continued. "This isn't chaos. In all forms of psychosis there will be some element of chaos. He is not psychotic.

That doesn't mean he is less dangerous. And he seems to be travelling around the country? One man whose face is all over the papers? That would mean he isn't all over the country. Soon he will hole up in one place unable to move, which means the plans for the next targets are either in place or soon to be so. You really need your sister." She looked directly at me. The Inspector's ears twitched. I inwardly sighed. She turned to the boss.

"Moo has an eye for detail, an obsession with faces, she can see patterns where others see chaos. She at the moment has plenty of time to trawl through all these sightings and establish a pattern. She may also be able to determine where he has been that you don't already know about."

My mother had continued oblivious to the politics of the office. Actually probably not oblivious. She chose to ignore them. Mum did not suffer fools gladly. Didn't suffer fools at all. She had frequently told my dad to grow up when he took offence at a tongue lashing. Deserved, probably as it was, her tongue didn't mince words, got straight to the point with no garnish. My dad suffered most, us children next and even her patients. She was patient to a point and then out it came. Of all the sisters, Moo, her nickname from birth, was super intelligent but, in life, if it was too easy she couldn't be bothered. She was at this very moment people watching for the fun of it on the South Bank.

A phone call from our Mum the night before had brought her to London. Now she was whiling the time away by estimating how long, and in what manner, it would take her to pickpocket each tourist that walked by, phone or wallet hanging loosely in their clothing. The actual implementation was irrelevant. It was the preparatory work beforehand that mattered.

A group of Japanese tourists walked by chattering incessantly and comparing photos on their cameras as they walked. A Samsung was trying to leap itself out of a jeans pocket. Moo spotted it and then spotted another scout. A real pick pocket. She moved forward effortlessly, picked the pocket and with a broad smile on her face handed it back to the owner saying, "Excuse me sir, I think you dropped this."

The tourist, aghast and overjoyed one at the same time, thanked her effusively, his head bobbing up and down, his white teeth flashing beer stains and beer breath into her face.

She smiled a sweet butter wouldn't melt smile at the pro, turned on her heel and almost away. The call came seconds later. She answered.

"Sis?"

The positive response was immediate. At last, something of substance to get her teeth into. Life was boring at the best of times. Now at last was something worth getting up for. A time-limit to track down a man, a man who had killed no-one yet apparently was a danger to everyone. And now her mother was involved. Hey! What else did she have to do except watch Japanese tourists on the South Bank? Might as well help her little sister out of a fix. She might even get a free drink every now and then.

She was stuck at the Reception at Thames House arguing with some poor girl caught in the headlights of her obvious distaste. Broughton himself went down to bring her up, She gave her Mum a big hug and exclaimed, "Mum, it's good to see you." As she turned to me exclaiming, "Sis," Broughton eventually made the connection. The Greene girls were my sisters.

Broughton tried to calm himself, "Well, Mrs Greene, is it Mrs Greene?

"I use it for work. Ysella's dad, my second husband was a Priest and I kept my professional world separate."

A mumbled "Yes I'm sorry for your loss. ……………..You certainly made some beautiful and amazing daughters. Just daughters? Or are there more to come out of the closet?"

"I'm very proud of each of them," she said. And she meant it.

"So, back to our man." The crossing of personal and public was uncomfortable for me.

"I detect and it's only a surmise of course, he's struggling. He believes in the ideology but is struggling with the method. He is turning it into a game and is wanting to lose but each chapter will get harder for you. He is not a walkover, he has honour, loyalty. There is something. There is an uncomfortableness within him. Trauma would be an obvious answer? So in essence he's struggling, believing in the ideology and principles but struggling with the implementation. He's oscillating and overcompensating."

"I can't see him overcompensating." Broughton was inquisitive.

"He is, the Empire bombings first but now the game, the dialogue. He didn't need to do that. He's figured out the ending. If you want to stop him you need to get there first."

"Ask him how many chapters of this game there are and what they are." Broughton charged me.

"He won't tell you," Mum interjected. "Moo, you are to find where he has been since Ysella and he got off the plane from Turkey."

Moo sighed. "There's money in it for you," Mum bribed.

Broughton went pale.

"It's alright, Mr Broughton, I will pay. I gather you've already been fleeced once this week by three of my daughters."

Broughton tried not to let the relief show and disappeared to a bank of monitors.

"Gatwick." You needed to warm to Moo before you got sentences. I had tried to warn Wilson as they walked away. He seemed like a lap dog being rejected by his master. He didn't hear. Didn't want to, I guess. He was transfixed. So many people had been. Moo appeared to be made of strong stuff, but it was her protective shell.

"Ahead of you." Wilson smiled and brought up the picture of Baydar at Passport Control.

"And…..?" Moo was baiting him.

"Ah, well."

Her disappointment was tangible. At the first hurdle he had let her down.

"The obvious place would be the car rentals. But he didn't go to any of them. So, the Gatwick Express? No. So, taxi rank? Bus rank? No."

"He can't just vanish. So," Moo thought out of the box all the time, "so, he never left Gatwick, except by plane."

"Tried that, checked all the flights. No Baydar was on any flight out of Gatwick. Why would it…….." Wilson trailed off. Moo caught his wavelength.

"Internal flights, because we know he is here."

"Okay ,check the British Airways stands."

They toured the British Airways ticket booths.

"Nothing."

"EasyJet." Wilson was excited. Moo was yet to be impressed.

Moments later she was, "Bingo."

"Now where was he going?"

"Let's assume first flight out. Because he didn't hang around. Straight from Passport Control to buy a ticket." He tapped away at the keyboard.

"Bingo." It was his turn.

"Not yet a full house." She looked at him and allowed herself to soften, "Edinburgh." It seemed to Wilson that she was purring.

"Gretna Green."

"One piece of a jigsaw we already know. Now where to after that?"

They scoured the terminal images of Edinburgh for the rest of the day. They assumed that Baydar left the terminal and were looking for his return. They hadn't bothered getting the name. They assumed if he could change passports once he could do so again. It was as Moo was running through this thought process out loud once more it dawned on them in unison.

"Of course."

Wilson put into words what they both knew to be true. "If he changed passports there is no reason why he can't change airports. But hang on, he would have needed time in Edinburgh or somewhere to prepare the Gretna bombing."

"Actually that doesn't matter, we know he was there. We need to know where he was going after that. We need to know the future venues."

"Yes, I can see that." Wilson was used to belt and braces, tying up all loose ends, creating a picture and therefore he would have liked to have got the information. He did, though, recognise that time was of the essence and Moo was right. Their job was to determine the next locations as soon as they could. He typed in Glasgow, gave himself a window of two days and after the third cup of takeaway coffee brought in by Jacintia with a wink and a smile each time, they found him.

"Time," said Moo. She noted it and clicked away on her phone.

"I'd guess if he sticks to the same format, East Midlands Airport."

Moments later. "Bingo." Wilson was about to call through to Broughton when Moo placed her hand on his shoulder. He shuddered.

"Doesn't really give us a location does it? Let's see if he returns to it first, and when."

Wilson acknowledged it. And they sat there almost blinded by faces traversing a thankfully small concourse. Each day covered was taking hours.

Eventually bleary eyed, Wilson conceded, "That is our cut off point, he doesn't return."

"How do you know?"

"Because two hours later he was having coffee with your sister in Exeter."

Broughton, my mum and I were pondering over where the location for power could be. The obvious Westminster for politics. The square mile for financial. GCHQ. Buckingham Palace. We were getting nowhere. We then decided to go down the theological routes to try to work out the next chapters. Creation, love, power……

We had a long list.

Sin, resurrection, faith, redemption, reconciliation, the fall, ten commandments, action, judgement, sin, damnation, salvation, forgiveness, incarnation, ascension, Kingdom of Heaven.

Mum had been nipping out at frequent times getting us supplies and popping in on Moo and Wilson. On the third occasion she came back, smiled and said, "I think your Mr Wilson has brought the soft side out of Moo. You've got sin down twice."

I was wide eyed through tiredness.

By this point I was now cross referencing places with the list of theological principles but actually, other than love and creation hadn't got further.

"Ok you two, I want you tell us what you've got."

Moo and Wilson joined Broughton as he had instructed.

They looked at the map and the pins. Broughton handed Wilson coloured wool.

"Best I had," Jacintia ventured. I looked quizzically at her.

"Maybe one day grandchildren from one of you. I was born for it."

Moo started to speak as Wilson threaded the wool around the pins of the known locations of Baydar.

"So, Liam, please start at Gatwick."

I was somehow surprised. Wilson's first name was Liam? Maybe Mum was right. Had Wilson tamed the monster?

"So we've got Gatwick to Edinburgh to Gretna to Glasgow to East Midlands airport. Another strand please. Then we have him twice at Exeter, Exeter to Norwich. We have him at Heathrow before that, Newcastle, Southampton"

"We think the rest must be by car sir." Wilson exclaimed.

"We've covered the airports because he has done this so quickly."

"Right, your turn," said Broughton. I stood up with my Post It notes. Well, what we know is of the theological doctrines we have, Creation is at Eden, Love is at Gretna. But as for the rest...."

I placed the Post It notes we had not used on the table. We gathered round.

We tried placing different names to different locations.

"Okay just stop for a second." Mum was tired. "Think like a religious person. Ysella think like your dad. Think of his liturgies."

The word was like a punch in the stomach that winded me. She hadn't spoken about Dad for a year.

"Ysella." The way my mum named me brought me back to reality and at the same time to my childhood.

"Okay, okay."

She wanted me to focus. She was a professional woman and now she was involved totally.

"Wilson, you got to East Midlands and there is a gap before you picked up the thread again. Name places around that area and shout them out, maybe something will resonate."

Nothing came.

Broughton exploded after sometime. Thumping his fist on the table. "Wilson, I'll send you to Coventry." The Olde English idiom to ostracise someone.

"That's it!" I had it.

"What?" The mutterings would have been a bit more excited if we all weren't so tired. "Well it is a chapter. Remember frequently Dad used the Litany of Reconciliation that was written after World War Two. It is symbolic of Coventry." A small victory. Not the next chapter, we have to figure out power first, but we could get to Coventry and try to dismantle the basic explosive device and maybe demonstrate to the public there was no terror, that everything was alright.

"You two. Birmingham airport, I want to know if he was there, and where from." Moo and Wilson started to leave.

"Now power." Broughton was invigorated or was it just the coffee?

"Power?" Wilson turned. "Religious power?"

"We've got Lambeth Palace on the list," I said.

"No, wrong. This is a power struggle between religion and secularism in essence isn't it?" Wilson asked.

"I suppose so." I was trying to see the thread.

"Think of your history. The power struggle between Church and State in the 12th century." We all stared blankly.

"Henry II and Thomas Becket. State versus Church and the Church lost. Becket was killed. You know, 'Who will rid me of this troublesome Priest?'"

Of course, a Bishop had used that phrase to my dad, who had then deflected it with the author of the quote, book and every detail until the Bishop conceded, just to get rid of him from the office.

"Canterbury," Broughton gasped.

It was almost as if he knew we had figured out where to go. We had barely reached the Old Kent Road when the email pinged.

"Power. By rights historically you should be travelling to Rome, right? The Church has wielded power and control. Crushing normality with a code of ethics based on itself rather than love. Love is forgiving, isn't it? The Church isn't. Let's start at the beginning. But let's use signs again. The Rainbow, a sign of God's covenant. Then the invisible God made visible in the burning bush. But then circumcision, the sign of them and us, superiority, yet supplanted by Christ with whom he was explicit, there was no hierarchy, in fact the last shall be first. In Christ, the ultimate and final sign, the invisible love of God made visible, now we see in a mirror darkly, then we shall see face to face. This incarnational love is

where power is relinquished.

I have read your Endo, I read the Samurai because I saw myself as a bit of a soldier. The more I read the more I identified myself with the man who was continuously used and abused. Who was satisfied but driven by others to achieve a task that can't be achieved."

I wanted to send a message back saying 'so don't continue' but I just read.

"The Samurai met the elders of the Church in Rome. As you say, Caiaphas rather than Christ. Everything that is wrong, trying to prop up a failing structure for its own sake. The Christian faith is an incarnational faith, therefore it doesn't ask for signs, you are correct but what it does do is make the invisible love of God visible. Love is vulnerable. We have already ascertained, have we not, that love costs? Therefore in your faith you are not creating anything, discovering anything, it isn't anything new, rather you are simply illuminating and science and theology go hand in hand in this role. It describes what is, that it may be best understood. Creation for some is a visible sign of God's love and yet how many notice the flower as it blooms anew. The Catholic Church and its little sister the Anglican Church have sacraments, do they not? Visible signs of invisible presences, to put it crudely. Remember the story of the Emmaus road, their eyes were opened when he broke bread. The sacrament is a sign that reminds us of what we are looking for, it isn't a sign to prove it is there. The Church though has lost this sense of wonder of the journey. It claims to be right. The second it starts to think like that it becomes them and us. Mission is them and us. It needs to feel itself in the world, of the world. Now, I know Christ didn't quite say that but Christ did not mean for anything like Church structures to exist. And when the Church does something, does it need to prove that it is doing good? Yes! 'Look what we do' it says. It needs to act for it is driven to respond to

*Christ's call. It sees it as essential, not seeing it as a good deed but a necessary deed of which there would be no comment. Where in the power of the Church is someone saying 'Lord, I believe, help thou my unbelief?' Where in the Church is someone bearing all things, believing all things, hoping all things, and enduring all things, simply because they understand that love, not power, is Christ's way. Love unites intrinsically. Power divides. My fear is that people only unite when they have a common enemy. The advent of strong right wing conservatism, where normal people think it is okay to talk about **them,** and keeping **them** out as if somehow entitlement to a piece of land is based on where we were born and what we inherit. Think about it, seriously, as Christians, where do you believe you seek unity, that there is no distinction between people; not by race or creed? Yet suddenly when our own exalted position is threatened we think it is ok. The Old Testament is littered with commandments to help the orphan, the homeless, the refugee (it is called stranger in the Old Testament.) In fact the children of Israel were in themselves refugees who had nothing and they came and took what they needed. Who are we to say that others cannot take food and land that they may live as we live. If we don't want it to happen then we have to look at how we can solve the problem. Do we blockade the Channel so no-one can get across or do we help those countries invest in themselves, grow prosperity, that this island doesn't seem quite the paradise it does from afar? We can't expect to take from the rest of the world their natural resources to profit our own pockets and not expect them to do the same, especially if they are far hungrier than we are.*

You have to come together, we have to work together, not demanding division but creating unity. Yes there are differences, but actually there are bigger differences over attitude, temperament and personality than there are biological differences in pigmentation or theological differences in religions. There is more that unifies humanity than there is that divides it. Remember from your biology class days, we are more related to the whale than the whale is to the shark.

93% of our DNA is a monkey's

90% of our DNA is a mouse's which explains why they are used in chemical research so much.

80% is a dog.

65% is a chicken.

The only way the world will survive is if you unify, join together, celebrating our differences and not letting them divide us. And yet the world is becoming more and more right wing- the selfish creed of 'what is in it for me?' is pervading the world.

No scapegoating. Scapegoats break the unity one by one. If we turn our world into 'them and us' it is doomed to fail because in the end someone will have what the other wants, and Hell will ascend as one side fights to keep what they have whilst the other side has nothing to lose in trying to get it. When the situation arises that that commodity is food, we have lost all hope. And yet, how close are we, look at the food-banks here. I can't believe that in this so called civilised society food banks are mainstream.

Politics is all about trying to find the unity and when politics fails then history shows us that it fails badly, and 19,000 innocent people can die in a day 100 years ago at the Somme.

So what can you do? We are together, we must find a common vision. We must work together, and find ways of working together even with those with whom we inherently disagree. We are more closely related to them than the whale is to us, and the whale is to the shark. It may be hard, we may find some other people's views abhorrent or naive. Demonstrate that which unites us, else we will demonstrate more clearly that which unties us. A small change of an i and a t moving places, but in a DNA sequence that is all it takes to create a new world.

This is the unity the Church should talk about. This is the power it should demonstrate to lead. So what concerns the Sunday Christian? What do Christians see as their symbols of the Church authorities? Big buildings emitting power."

Mum read the email in the back of the car with me.

"Although I can see where he is coming from, this is extreme, he is on the verge, he is swapping openly between using 'you' and 'we' so there are some issues of identity as I guess we would expect. You, Ysella, can alter the course of events. We know reconciliation is coming at some point, something he is probably sure about. The fact he is extreme means he is uncomfortable. You need to make this personal; bring the softer side out. Remember also he is Turkish."

My look asked for clarification.

"With the onset of modern Western society, countries like Japan, India managed to hold onto their roots. They developed, merged and modernised but at heart the culture remained the same. Turkey did not. It threw out Islam as a force in the state and embraced Western modernism with both arms. An extreme reaction some would say but of course it went unnoticed in the West because we thought they were doing the right thing. Baydar is trying to make the world, or actually this country, do what Turkey did but he doesn't seem to understand it. His is at a slightly off centre ideological standpoint."

"Except he is not Baydar," said Broughton glancing up from another email.

"Grantham has sent a brief report. Basically they found the chalet at Kabak."

"Kabak?" interjected my mother.

"Long story," I intervened.

Broughton continued. "Across the whole place was enough medical equipment and medicines to fight a small war. They found evidence of an operating theatre and bits and pieces to perform plastic surgery. They've found litres of blood stored, not Baydar's blood type. They've found surveillance equipment in what was in a makeshift sickroom and also sound equipment. There were books on Russian, French, English, Turkish. There was music on an iPod which consisted of the Earth Song by Jackson and the Man in the Mirror. Lennon's Imagine. Cat Steven's Morning has Broken. Satchmo's What a Wonderful World."

There were a few blank looks.

"Satchmo, Louis Armstrong."

Nods of comprehension.

"Dylan's Blowing in the Wind, War by Edwin Starr, Marley's Redemption Song and Change is Going to Happen by Sam Cooke, amongst others," Broughton concluded.

"Common theme," a voice came from somewhere in the room, echoing the thoughts of all.

"It will take months of negotiation with the Turkish authorities to get the full picture but my hunch is he isn't Baydar. But whether our man knows that, who knows? Broughton shrugged in resignation.

"You have the connection, Lella," I heard my mum say. "Use what you know, keep it personal."

I typed.

"My dad wasn't like that, my dad wrestled as I told you. So do those above him, they don't find it easy. None of them would have fought for something that was corrupt, they all believed the Church could be a moment of change but also

recognised its frailties in the world. Some of his superiors stuck their neck out for him, some of his colleagues stabbed him in the back. All recognised his gifts, all his weaknesses. The Church structures are there to support the weak. The Church no longer claims any moral high ground. The Church is its people not its buildings. So if you want to bomb Canterbury, it should be the Archbishop not the Cathedral. And those people have clearly demonstrated they are servants, deacons.

Christians believe that we are the Easter people, that is the essence of our faith in hope. For us to understand the concept of hope in our daily lives we need to be as children. In my childhood Christmas was the perfect time. The reality of the Christmas story is not the promise of redemption in some after-life, it is about hope here in the very precious present. (Deliberate pun) At Christmas time, people hear more about the stories of Jesus. Those stories in which there is a bias to the poor, the woman who lost her family and got given back her son. The lowliest of the low, the shepherds, an integral part of the story. Jesus listened and gave importance to those members of society who had no voice, the non-people. The outcast and the foreigner were the first at the stable. Jesus with his miracles gave hope to those dispossessed by the then civilised society. And without hope we lose courage to be who we are. There will always be someone better yet you are the answer to someone's prayers. Dad made me understand the Niemöller quote, summarised thus:

When they came for the communists, the dissenters, the Trade Unionists and the Jews I kept quiet because I wasn't one. So when they came for me, there was no one to speak up for me.

This is the world we want to change. Not through terror. Each Priest takes the needs of the day and expresses them liturgically. I will be the first to admit some of my dad's colleagues get it wrong but that isn't deliberate, it is just because we all have different ideas about what is going on in the world and how to express it. If the heart, soul, love and care behind the liturgy is not expressed, instead the words are just repeated in monotone, then liturgy becomes meaningless at best or some kind of bizarre magic at worse. Whatever we do, in liturgy, in study, in caring for others, we should be facilitating encounters with the divine reality. But how often do we follow procedures and rituals for the very sake of those procedures and rituals.

My dad lambasted what happens on a Sunday; in particular the sermon.

An outdated method of doing theology, it nevertheless tries to help us encounter God by using the bizarre process of explanation. You know the Bible. Reading the Gospels without any knowledge of the socio-economic background of Israel actually renders a lot of the stories open to misinterpretation, and yet most do our theology in that very vacuum. Does it matter? That is just one aspect, the complexities of theology are layered so deeply and woven with many different strands it is difficult to hold in balance all the many conflicting elements on our journey of encounter towards God. It actually means that our theology behind the initiation ceremonies of baptism and confirmation and reception into communion need to develop, because behind these protocols is the desire for the establishment to know that people have knowledge. This therefore excludes many people of faith, who for whatever reason have limited understanding in their faith. It excludes small children and others who cannot grasp intellectual principles of faith. Who does, in reality? Who does understand our faith? As you say, our faith should be one desire that says 'I believe. Help thou my unbelief,' rather than 'I believe this because I know that.' Therefore we cannot and should not turn anyone away because they do not know or do not understand, God just requires us to say 'Yes Lord...' To offer what we have in the words of the child with the loaves and the fishes. The boy did not sit down and work out what would happen, he didn't think how can my lunch feed everyone? He just said, this is what I have, it is yours.

Of course it doesn't stop there. That is just the self offering, that is what brought us all here at the beginning, what happens next, that is discipleship. There are three stages of discipleship and I personally think that in each of us they occur in different orders. These stages are belief, belonging and behaving. Some people believe first, then belong to the body of believers and then this effects their behaviour. Others have the behaviour, then belong, then come to believe. Others believe, then belong, then behave. Yet others believe, then behave, then belong. In reality, I would surmise, we move back and forth between them all at various stages. So what happens next as we grow in all three? As Christians we have a variety of tools to broaden our knowledge of our encounters with God. We have of course the Bible, our creeds, our liturgies, our own experience and consciousness as we interact with those around us and the wider world. To use these tools we need reflection, space and then the desire to set our journey within a context. A context of ourselves, our community and family, our history and the stories that have made us, and then the stories of the Church. Is this why you are in your mission? Is it because you are not rooted in your own identity? You don't know who you are, do you? You have no story? That is why you can separate yourself from what you are doing! On top of that our life encounters pose new problems and new questions as the complexities of life call on us to re-question and refresh ourselves in the light of new global problems.

The most basic intrinsic question we have to ask ourselves is: What is God calling us to do?

Obey? Love?

How about dance? Dance where we may learn steps but actually it isn't about the rules of dance, it is about enjoying the music. For instance you can learn a two step by using the waltz count. To dance purists this is anathema, for to the purist you should learn the dance by learning the dance, not by changing it to fit. In our sphere we have to change and adapt to try to make sense of it all, to try to make it work. The doctrines, the liturgies are there to help us not control us. Our faith is about our communion with God, not the doctrines, sacraments, rules and stipulations just as the importance of a dance is to enjoy it. If you don't enjoy the dance don't bother dancing, if you don't commune with God then don't use a religion. In Ephesians, Paul tells us that Christ forms a new humanity where there is no distinction between those circumcised and uncircumcised, but all are one in the household of God with Christ as the cornerstone.

So our worship, our prayers should be liberating us into the joy of God, a communion that should be like a dance. We then hold onto the end result, our communion with the divine reality. We need to let go of the rituals, else sometimes we find ourselves worshipping the ritual and not communing with God.

Christianity shouldn't be ritual, more about the journey and recognising our weakness on that journey. A pilgrimage if you like, reminiscent of Chaucer. This is our pilgrimage, I guess, and it is the journey as opposed to the destination that is important. Correct?" Send.

Mum put her hand gently on mine and squeezed. Her face became the "well done" face of my childhood. This was not a time to be demonstrative.

We waited. We had reached the M2 and the driver was accelerating, covering the ground to Canterbury quicker than the train from Victoria would have done.

Just outside of Canterbury there was a diversion which took us through the quaint village of Harbledown. This is where Henry II stopped to visit the lepers on his pilgrimage from London after Becket's death. As we merged on the other side my phone pinged. Broughton gestured for the driver to stop. He pulled over two wheels on the pavement.

I read it to everyone in the car.

"Becket window on the sill. Cut the blue wire and it will be safe."

Broughton was on his phone gesturing to the driver to turn round and take us back to Thames house. Others were being called in as there was no point in our presence, we now had to work out what was next. We didn't have to wait long. Ping.

"Faith."

"Great," said Broughton, "I failed R.E. at school."

"S'all right, Mr Broughton, so did my husband."

Faces turned to look at my mum aghast, including mine. She simply smiled, she delighted in keeping others on their toes.

Chapter Ten- Faith and Resurrection

When we listen to someone do we hear the whole story? We don't. We hear the parts of the story that resonate more. Those that are a bit more salacious, more exciting maybe than the everyday mundane lives that so many live. So many in the West thrive on someones else's gossip that becomes part of their story but isn't theirs at all. Look at Facebook, Instagram, Snapchat.

The whole story often includes pain and heartache, joy and liberation. It is full of paradoxes pulling in all directions at once. It is a story of one person viewed many different ways and that person viewing the world many different ways. We are changed by what we hear, by what we see. Our experiences of life make us who we are and yet no one sees the whole story; the nuances and reflectiveness are missed in the quest for yes or no, black or white, false or truth. See the person behind the speaker. See which words come from the heart but if you just use the cerebral you lose the vulnerability. How many words are spoken for the heart and not the head and how many words are lost because of it. Our stories are never told and yet elements of them are to suit the story teller. Who tells the story now, what is our story, what is our faith story? Whose story do we tell and to whom? Whose stories are within our story? Supplement our story and who's story will our story supplement and be held within?

It was Mum's idea to change things around. Rather than wait for his email I would start. After all, the tables had been turned once already. Now was the time to gain some strategic advantage. I typed whilst I was driven.

"On the night before he died, Jesus, through the blessing, breaking and sharing of bread, told part of the story of Moses and then he made that story part of his story giving it new meaning. He said, "It is my body." Less than twenty fours later that meaning became clear, the veil of unknowing was torn and the Holy of Holies was seen clearly. A story of sacrifice for the stories of his friends, his enemies and the many who were to come.

Now this story is retold and therefore the stories of Moses are retold and the stories of the theologians and simple folk down the years. Their story is your story and we tell their story because it has meaning. It had meaning then and has meaning now. Different language must be a priority in the retelling. It's retelling needs to be subjected through the prism of today. It isn't gossip with which to titillate a drab existence but is a story full of light and grace and redemption. All stories are interlinked. The incarnation. Redemption. Salvation. These themes are there in our daily lives. Faith therefore is there, whether we like it or not. Faith sometimes needs structure and that is religion. It keeps us from megalomania. The stories therefore help us to see life as universal. What does this mean? This universalism of life? Our stories are so interwoven of past, present and future. We are all players in one universal story. What does that story mean? For Jesus, let he who is without sin cast the first stone.

Why inflict terror on the innocent when they are no more different than us. For faith, even faith in humanity, please stop." Send.

A bit blunt. I was tired and had exhausted myself on the trip down. I just wanted to close my eyes. Moo and Wilson had stayed behind and had received the next topic immediately we knew it. When we slipped onto the M25 heading west, I looked up into the mirror. Broughton was looking for the eye contact.

"Base camp suggest the multi faith room at Heathrow. Apparently it is well used by those who require faith to get onto a tin can and fly at 20,000 feet. It also makes sense as our man has lived in airports which is where the idea could have come from. Also we may have some DNA results from Kabak in the next seventy two hours if we are lucky."

As soon as he had finished my phone pinged.

"Interesting line of thought. I assume you know where you are going. So, this is about the church, not Jesus. The Church's birthday is Pentecost. This marks the clear transfer from knowledge to faith. After the resurrection the disciples were looking back. Their present was defined by their past. Much of our world is defined by the past. What we can and cannot do is defined by atrocities of the past. Laws are created for these reasons. Understandable, not healthy. Don't put the hand to the plough and look back. Ask Lot. Pentecost tells us look to the future. The future is change, accept what needs to be done, this is faith."

My dad would have agreed with it so far. I had his notebooks with me. I found some notes and balancing the pages open for reference I typed-

"Pentecost tells us to mindfully live in the moment. It is about living in the moment that truly God is of the living. God is of the here and now, for the message is within us if only we would stop and feel it. Faith and life are about truly living in the moment. Tolle says that if we accept who we truly are that doesn't mean accepting the status quo but change is indeed inevitable not out of fear, rather out of a sense of pure naturalness. Christians spend their lives praying and more often than not they are praying for change, change of illness, change of weather. Dad used a phrase that prayer was 'the unquantifiable body language of the soul.' Our soul cannot be anything but part of God's presence and we need to listen."

Send. Ping.

"Very nice and thoughtful. Don't confuse faith with Church is my point. The two are arguably mutually exclusive most if not all of the time. That is what needs to change. Get rid of all religion and we may lose some but we will gain more of the spiritually faithful. You can't disagree with that. The link between religion and culture in the West needs to start again. Everyone needs to be kick started away from these institutions and recognise their faith."

I started typing immediately.

"The Church has its place, it was at the beginning when all it had was faith. Yes in some respects the institution is maintained but that is because the institution can evolve once more and revolutionise itself back to its core values."

Send. There was a pause and I could feel my heart beating in my chest.

Ping

"They tried that at the reformation. Martin Luther's articles nailed to a door and look where we are now."

I was typing as I read, *"Isn't that simply humanity?"* Send. Ping.

"So we need Noah."

Broughton was tapping into his phone. I heard a voice answer on the other end and Broughton's exasperation as he spoke.

"Ok, so where is the multi faith room at Heathrow, Wilson? Wilson?" Broughton was shouting into the phone. Then he went silent and stared transfixed at it.

"Which one?" came the answer.

Broughton was dumbfounded.

"Before or after security?" Wilson continued

"It is over to you to find out and stop this thing, Heathrow of all places," he tapered off. "Just sort it, all of you." He rubbed his eyes. I hadn't realised how tired he looked.

"No pressure then." I murmured.

Mum broke me out of my thoughts. "Send those emails to Filippa, I've already told her to expect them. She knows Heathrow like the back of her hand. Maybe there is a clue in them of which room we need to go to. I dutifully did, more as a loss for an alternative than simply obeying Mum.

Seconds passed and the reply came back which was obvious in the cold light of day.

I read it and to myself smiled, "Of course."

"Thanks sis."

"St George's chapel, a specifically Christian chapel, because this is against the Church now, not all religions, isn't it. There is something personal with the Church, he said it himself." There were a lot of connections pulsating in my brain and I parked them on the side concentrating on the present.

I typed, *"St Georges Chapel between 2 and 3."* Send. Ping.

"Well done." Ping. *"It doesn't change anything yet though."*

"Shit." I was louder than I intended. I was ignored. Perhaps they knew that I hadn't done enough yet. Where do you start with faith? Faith. Faith? I was better with love I think, or more likely hope. Okay, let's start with faith, hope and love, and the greatest of these is love. But we've done love. I was tapping on my phone trying to make connections. I stopped. Rifled through my bag and found another notebook. I leafed through the pages and found what I wanted. I typed, paraphrasing the text in front.

"We are told that faith, hope and love are the greatest gifts in the world and the greatest of these is love. Love drives us to achieve the unachievable, to reach

out and grasp the ungraspable. Hope keeps us going when logic and rationality say give up. Faith inspires the other two. For faith has no reason behind it, faith is unreasonable. It makes no sense. But then love makes no sense, and hope is very often illogical. Faith in others, faith in believing others. Faith has an element of trust. Every member of the armed forces who are asked by us to lay their lives on the line hourly, because don't forget the battle is no longer on the battlefield of France, or in the theatre of war in Afghanistan, the battle ground is here on our streets. The murder of Lee Rigby demonstrates that for 24 hours a day British service women and men have to be wary for their own safety and the safety of their families. It is back to the days of the 70's and 80's with the conflict in Northern Ireland."

Send. I waited. Ping.

"The problem is when we remember war it is most often over there. You are right, war is here, right now. The question we have to ask ourselves is, do we want a better world? Can we make that world happen? Or do we sit back and just accept what it is? So how can we make change happen?"

I started typing immediately.

"If you have faith believing change can happen you will be a part of that change. 100 years ago one of the world's most significant moments that would change the face of the world occurred. The almost bloodless Bolshevik revolution passed by unnoticed in St Petersburg where it happened; citizens continued to eat in restaurants, to go to the theatre and 40 years later 1/3 of the population of the world lived under Lenin-inspired constitutions."

Send

I wasn't myself sure of where the argument was going, but I had to find faith. I thought history would maybe conjure up a few clues. Could GCSE history come to my aid? Ping.

"Of course. History dictates that the communist ideals of Marx and Engels were soon lost in the politics of power and within seven years the apparatus for a totalitarian regime was in place. The reason for the transformation in Russia, the democratic election to power of Hitler and Mussolini is because normal people were suffering in the previous regime and they held out hope for a better future and used that hope through faith to bring about peaceful change. That is fine if the Government of our country serves the will of the majority. Of course what you are seeing with Brexit and all the issues surrounding it is then the minorities are picked upon. Democracy is dangerous because in the end it is self seeking. But change can happen if people want it enough. There is a second major event that occurred almost simultaneously as the Russian Revolution; the Balfour declaration that stated that Britain would back the establishment of a Jewish homeland in Palestine. Significant change and arguably one that has had a profound affect on Middle Eastern stability since. Change because people wanted it enough and people power won. "

Now I wasn't in the debate to argue, I felt we were somehow on the same side and I wanted to know more. A quest for knowledge if you like. *"That is why when it comes to war, politicians try to tell us it is in our interests to go to war. Except for Chamberlain and history remembers him as a weak, naive idealist."* Send. Ping.

"History remembers wrong. One of his aids at the time has said that the piece of paper was a political tool. Either it was a valid promise of Hitler in which case it was invaluable, or it wasn't and it became invaluable in demonstrating to the Americans just what Hitler was really like, and therefore would drag them in to any war that Chamberlain had predicted would be coming. The country was in a no lose situation, peace on the one hand or the Americans as allies on the other. Unfortunately for Chamberlain history meant he was always going to lose."

I wanted to return now to try to stop everything. I pondered.

"We have faith, hope and love and we can change the world because we give that faith, hope and love into the hands of politicians, and by politicians I also mean those in the hierarchy of the Church. We choose them whether for Parliament or Church. Then it all goes wrong. These are the very last people we should be exposing our vulnerability to. So your fight isn't against normal people who are the ones who are frightened. Your fight is against those whom you'll never touch." Send. Ping

"Those who have died in armed conflict don't die for politicians, they died for us their relatives and future generations. They gave their love to us and we gave our hope and faith to them. It is a reciprocal relationship."

Adrenalin pulsed through me.

"That is where Christianity comes in. It is a religion based on reciprocity through covenant. It teaches us that unless there is this mutual vulnerability then things are going to go wrong. When it all goes wrong is when there is no vulnerability in politics. You can help us to change not by terror but by persuasion!"

Send. Ping

"Politicians are saying that British people who have fought alongside IS in Raqqa will die in Raqqa. Politicians are denying them the British rights of a trial by jury, innocence before guilt. Maybe they have no choice. I am not a politician but what I will say this, if they adopt this attitude then how dare they criticise other countries, my country, when my Government is forced to adopt a similar attitude to their enemies of the state. It is hypocrisy on a genocidal scale."

I could not really argue. So I continued what was now our line of thought.

"The guiding principles to a Christian's life are faith, hope and love. They

maintain us in times of hardship and in times of plenty they should govern our decisions. Whatever befalls us, whatever our friends have to do and face, if we govern all that is within our decision making process by using the principles faith hope love we can change the world for the better and hopefully fewer people will be damaged by war. The world has changed most dramatically not by terror or coup d'etat, but peasants, workers, bourgeoisie and the gentry coming together and peaceably saying enough is enough. This is faith." Send. Ping.

"Resurrection."

Broughton breathed a sigh of relief. "Ok crisis averted." I typed.

"Where do we find the explosive?" Send. Ping.

"Don't worry, by the end of the day or the week it will be in a landfill site. Depending on how often the chaplain empties his bin. It is safe til then."

I forwarded this email to Broughton who informed someone. Two wins, I mused, and then returned to the brainstorming session ensuing around me.

We were closing in on Thames House. Before we had taken the first slurp of the hot fluid MI5 called coffee inside, Broughton was speaking.

"Brainstorm everyone, we are not stopping until this is sorted. When I say resurrection what are the words that come to mind?"

"Christ."

"Jesus."

"Ok, so where are the places we associate with Resurrection?" he was clueless but hyper.

"Jerusalem."

"William Blake, Jerusalem, satanic mills."

"Yes I like that. Wilson, chase it up, see if you can get anything."

Silence. Ping.

"Let the games commence," Broughton was almost bouncing off the walls.

"He's watched too much Hunger Games with his daughters," Wilson whispered under his breath. Moo giggled.

Broughton was buoyed by the success and behaved like the child who believed he was on the winning team without understanding the game.

I read the email.

"Ok, listen up he's just asked whether the resurrection happens nowadays? Broughton appealed.

I imagined tumbleweed drifting across the room.

Mum broke the silence, "Text your sister, Sapphire, she is eerily literal. She'll know. Text Ruby too, you never know."

The texts from the twins came back very quickly and only seconds apart. I read Sapphire's to myself, *"You mean like caterpillars into butterflies, and stuff?"*

Ruby was more self assured. *"Resurrection, or new life, happens across nature. In Europe, trees and flowers grow and die in the seasons. Then you have water-bugs that grow into dragonflies and caterpillars that grow into butterflies. In fact the butterfly is the symbol of new life."*

'Got it,' I whistled.

"The butterfly, the symbol of new life. Moo can you find paintings, sculptures, anything like that currently in the UK? …………..Please?"

She smiled. As the next oldest to me she had spent my toddler years telling me to say please and thank you.

Everybody seemed to be industrious. My mum had disappeared but was to come back later, phone in hand.

Moo was working on Butterflies with Liam. They had a strong bond. I guess with Jenkins and Grantham still slaving away in Turkey, at least that was what they had reported back although they had little tangible evidence as yet, Liam Wilson had found an ally who wasn't a competitor. They had a bond that knew a strong depth. Like they had been in the same class at school or something.

"Ok we've got the butterfly museum in London and one in Glasgow. Both are distinct possibilities," Liam ventured.

"Also, and my favourite, one from the Van Gogh butterfly collection in the National Gallery." Moo was sending a piercing look my way as she said it.

Broughton made the call to Glasgow. Moo and Wilson were given the National Gallery with Broughton and I the Natural History Museum, Kensington. We went by Tube which I took as an explanation for why the email didn't come through. I logged into the wifi at the museum. Nothing. We waited for an hour and despite my anxiety which was hitting high levels on all scales, PHQ9 or GAD7, I actually managed to appreciate some of the exhibits. Broughton was on the phone to Wilson and to Glasgow. Nothing there. Wilson had managed to get the museum closed temporarily for maintenance by accidentally flooding one of the toilets on an upper floor. Those who saw the water accepted the explanation without question and were no doubt enjoying a latte in a nearby cafe trusting the museum would be open in an hour. Broughton was impressed. Colleagues were now scouring the place for any small device. The Glasgow Police department had stormed in and had caused a minor furore but found nothing.

Two hours had gone and nothing. Not anywhere.

"Damn." Broughton was controlling his feelings, his frustrations, his tiredness.

He dialled into the phone and unceremoniously murmured, "Office."

He only spoke again when we were all assembled in Thames House.

"Is it butterflies or other?"

"Charles," my mum's voice would soothe the most ferocious of storms. Charles? Broughton's name? Wilson also turned in surprise.

"This is the suggestion of number one bambina." She passed her phone across the desk between them. I glanced at the screen and ascertained that there had been some ferocious texting between the two. The word that leapt out though was "Goldfinch." I knew the book by Donna Tart, Filippa had heavily recommended it. Dad had read it, it was a gift from Mum with the inscription by Jung on the inside written in her unique difficult to read to style. *"The meeting of two personalities is like the contact of two chemical substances: if there is any reaction, both are transformed."*

Broughton took off his glasses and frowned.

"I would never have got that, but actually does it put us any nearer knowing where?"

"Of course." Mum's charm felt like chocolate over truffles. "Now the most famous of paintings is, as you would know, Charles, by Fabricius which just happens to be at the National Galleries of Scotland in Edinburgh at the moment."

"My my, he had a busy time in Scotland. Hats off to you Mrs Greene. But why the Goldfinch?"

"Number one bambina says Herbert Friedmann."

She was reading another text that Filippa had sent through.

"He was a post-war ornithologist that identified the symbolic meanings of the Goldfinch as 'soul, sacrifice, death and resurrection.'"

She looked up. "My husband's death had a profound affect of Filippa. I know she has been doing a lot of reading around the subject lately."

He softened and replied, "Ok, so how do we handle it?"

"Same as last time?" My question was directed to my mum rather than the boss. He looked to her too. Broughton simultaneously picked up his phone and a coffee.

"Why not?" she shrugged. "Take the game to him. He hasn't responded so do something different."

"Just as marriage is to love, so funerals are to resurrection in the mind of the Christian. The classic funeral rite will include the Nunc Dimittis, the Song of Simeon. This moment in Christ's life is always seen as the goodbye of Simeon but it is actually the hello of Jesus. Hello to a new beginning, the change is already occurring. The King is dead, long live the King. Life is about holding the balance between hellos and goodbyes. The funeral rite is often the point of release from the hard few months that precede it. Life itself is full of goodbyes and hellos. That is the essence of Christianity. Death is broken, life is there to be grasped. It isn't about the yin and yang or every bad has a good. Rather the opportunities arise each time there is an ending. Chapters open and close, the very cycle of days, weeks, months and years is about ushering out the old and welcoming in the new. Each moment we look to the past is wasted. Each moment we dream of the future is wasted. Rather we work in the present which will form the future based on the achievements and challenges of the past. It becomes hard when the past looks rosier than the present or the future. It is hard but manageable when the future looks rosier than the present. All of us at one stage or another get stuck. As I see

it, Jesus on the cross is not saying, 'It'll be alright in the end'. Rather, he is focusing on the present: 'My God, why hast thou forsaken me?' 'Father, forgive them for they know not what they do.' That very moment, focused in the present. Nothing about, 'I take away your past sins.' Nothing about the 'future resurrection.' Only with the addition of theology and hindsight are we then able to give everything a past and a future. At that moment there was nothing but that moment. Too often we get embroiled in the planning and forget the living. We only have one moment to live and it is this one."

"Your dad would have been proud," she said.

"Should I send it?" The merest of nods confirmed it. I pressed the paper aeroplane and it whizzed away.

Broughton was finishing his phone-call. As he did so he handed a slip of paper to Wilson who responded by turning to his computer and keying in the directions that had been handed to him.

I glanced over and saw a live stream of the "Goldfinch" in Edinburgh.

"Saves the journey," he flatly exclaimed. Ping.

"The present moment for some can be unbearable. Life isn't always about happy endings, it can't be. The promise of the resurrection has been used by the Church to maintain the status quo. You are right. The moment of the now is the most special gift of life that we are given. What of the pain that determines no future? What of the past pains that cause the present painful moment of life? We cannot take away these questions of theodicy. For some the moment is too much to bear. What do we receive at these moments, trite and empty words? Don't try to contradict me. No explanation is enough to satisfy the questions of life. There is a story, or several stories really of a pilgrimage of very different souls to the Ganges. They each are searching for something, some meaning, some answer and

in very different ways they each find it. Otsu, the failed Priest, dies there because of the modern 'must have everything' approach to life of the young photographer in the party. The answers each of the pilgrims find are very different. Their pasts determine this moment. We are left at the end of the novel with as many questions as we had at the beginning. Questions are more important than the answers. The questions keep us journeying on our own individual pilgrimages. The moment we stop questioning is the moment we stop the pilgrimage, the moment we stop living. What did your Father think of the book?"

I looked at my mum quizzically as she read the email on the screen.

"Deep River," she said. "Endo. Your Dad loved it. In fact we even went to Toronto once so he could listen to some experts talk on it. He was like a child at Christmas. Ask your Mr Dalaman about Endo's Silence."

I typed, *"It was Dad's favourite. Tell me what of the 'Silence' of God in Endo's seminal work? Surely as he was a Catholic Christian you cannot stain us all with the same brush. He demonstrates a "better" more realistic faith?"*

Send. Ping.

"Very good, I am reading your Mr. Endo a lot. Thank you for sending his work across my bows. Now you will know that the Catholic Church kept Mr Endo at arm's length. It wasn't until Scorsese's film that they actually gave his work any credence. Did you know he is considered to be the greatest living novelist never to get the Nobel Prize. You see, Miss Ysella, I have been doing my homework. The Church though have chosen to ignore his real theology so still across the world people pray expecting God's intervention in human affairs. The sun shining on their daughter's wedding day. God intervening in war because somehow one side is right. Maybe you Christians who think the Church needs to become more real need to start saying so. One of those student pioneer sanctimonious people at Ravenscroft Park handed me a leaflet yesterday saying

how I needed to be saved by Jesus, accepting him as my personal saviour. So tell me, what is the point of the cross? If it was just for the few then what kind of faith is that? Your Mr Endo says that the true faith needs to be universal if it is to be real. For all people at all times. I know what St. Paul says but he was writing for the ordinary folk who could not hope to live up to the standards set by the Pharisees of which he had been a member. This justification by faith is severely lacking, because who has faith enough? Who has knowledge enough? Who is ever enough for anything? Jesus said be like children, no knowledge, no faith as such, simple trust. Trust in the Church, the face of Christ."

Here was my way in.

"In Endo's 'Silence', Rodriguez's journey is about seeing the face of Christ change. The King disappears and is replaced by the suffering servant. In 'The Samurai' too, it is the changing face of Christ that matters. This determines for us that our pilgrimage of faith is about discerning the true face of Christ, and it isn't the Church." Send. Ping.

"But God has no hands on earth but yours. No voice but yours. Your Church believes that but doesn't believe it to be the ultimate sacrifice, rather your Church is the very religious authority that Jesus criticised. Take the power away from the Church."

I laughed to myself.

"What power? I thought we'd done power?"

Send. Ping

"Oh it has power, look what I've done and I have no power."

It was true, Church attendance was up since the Empire bombings. There was something cultic about the faith that is used as the failsafe should logic and reason go wrong. Of course every priest in every part of the land was preaching something different. That is the beauty of

Christianity, context defines everything. Liberation theology, though ignored of late, was actually strong in essence if not in following.

"But the Church doesn't REALLY have power." Send. My futile, almost plaintive, attempt. Ping

"Answer me this. Does it preach the resurrection to give hope."

"Yes." Send. Ping.

"So why can't it preach the moment, the specialness?"

"Sometimes it does." Send. Ping.

"What is the predominant season that it celebrates?"

"Christmas." Send. Ping.

"Ah yes Christmas. At Christmas when bombs are being dropped in a far off land in the name of peace and a quest in the name of democracy and love. Where bombs are described as good progress. Coming to a world where countries negotiate boundaries, that some may live in splendour and keep those who have little outside. Where a news story today is a distant memory tomorrow.

Where in one small country, on one day 450 jobs are lost and it is cheaper to buy coal from thousands of miles away. Where livelihoods are cast aside and we progress, where progression is confined to the few based on the exploitation of the many. Christmas. In a world where the greatest democracy means citizens have the right to hold guns to take life and yet have to pay to save life. Where the world values a kick of a ball more than a life. When people live in fear, fear of being taken from their homes for having a contrary opinion.

A Christmas when scapegoats are found in those who are different, where we join together to conquer space and yet divide to exploit our scarce resources and destroy the planet.

When people's lives are subjected to gossip; where appearances rather than reality is what counts; where judgement is proclaimed and compassion a

weakness. Where we pray for Christmas to be lived every day and yet people strive for 15 mins of infamy over a lifetime of happiness.

Where people are silenced with threat and coercion and nights are dark and fearful. Where calmness is when you get what you want rather than stilling the mind when it is disappointed.

Where sleep for so many in civilised society is dependent on tranquilisers and pills. We need a world that reflects true Christmas. Where we wear each other's shoes, where we take risks to save lives, where love is made incarnate in today, and the precious moment is treasured for tomorrow, today should be a development of yesterday, where we learn from the mistakes of the past and recognise the futility of hate. For Christmas to mean anything we need to work for a world where all may sleep in peace, in hope, in safety, this night, that our hearts be stilled and hatred in whatever name is silenced. So how does that relate to Christmas presents, over-indulgence, debt and marital hardship. Christmas has lost all essence of meaning to the vast majority. Christmas is now more secular than anything."

Mum read it. "True. Now be softer. Tell the Christmas story in a way that will bring him in. Tell of the humanity of the Christmas story like Dad used to."

I looked at the screen and the years of listening, of being a part of the Christmas plays, the soup kitchen handouts all came back.

"A young woman quietly preparing for marriage. She was lucky her betrothed loved her. He was older and yet there was a bond between them. He worked hard, he cared for her, he loved her, and in the end that was all she needed. The housework, the continuum of dust, the fetching and carrying water, and endless struggle to make ends meet to get a week's meals out of one meal. This was her job. His to provide. His money meant they managed, he had a skill, his

hands were strong and dexterous, caring and persuasive. Callous yet gentle. Someone appeared before her, she was taken aback, she dropped the clothes she was repairing. Fear seized her and at that moment the angel said 'do not be afraid. Life changing events are to occur, but don't be afraid. Life will never be the same again, but don't be afraid. You can't control the future, let the changes occur, don't resist them you are part of them. Through you, new life will live. Do not be afraid. The joys and pains of new creation and joys and pains of bringing up a child, and pain of losing her son.'" Send. Ping.

"Go on."

He was a righteous man, he was happy, he was to marry this beautiful girl the apple of his eye, and yet the news she brought him. Unbelievable! Pregnant? How could she? What would the people think? To protect himself what could he do? Yet he loved her, he always said he would do anything for her. He wrestled and wrestled. His work slowed and mistakes crept into his normally robotic figures. He looked at the wood and his eyes were misted through tears. He desperately needed to sleep and finally he slumped over his wood. The emotion draining his every sinew. And he dreamt, a figure appeared before him, he had never seen anything like it. Fear seized him, and at that moment the angel said do not be afraid. Life changing events were to occur, but don't be afraid. Life will never be the same again. You can't control the future, let the changes occur, don't resist them, you are part of them. Through you new life will live. Do not be afraid. The sadness was intoxicating and yet he was asked to trust and have faith. He had a long journey ahead of him, literally and metaphorically and at the end would only be more wonder and more questions, but somehow it made sense." Send.

I took a deep breath, I needed time. Time to be more strategic. I was winging it. I needed a plan to draw him in, this was just the bait. Was it good enough? He was not stupid. Yet he wanted this. He wanted the dialogue. He was enjoying being changed. Ping.

"There are more characters in the story. We can't ignore the bad apples just because it suits us. What about them?"

I sighed. Herod! I cracked my fingers the way Dad used to to take the tension out of them when he had an idea that would mean he wouldn't look up from the computer keyboard for an hour or more. I typed.

"Supposedly it was another man controlling everything, a leader, a politician who sat atop of the pile. Change was afoot. It was terrifying. Not only did he sense it, those around him could feel it. Predicted in the stars if you like. He didn't like it, change wasn't good. He was benefiting. As did those psychopaths surrounding him. He was terrified. He could almost hear the people singing in his head, the people whose ideas he oppressed. 'It's been a long, long time coming But I know a change gonna come; Oh, yes it will.' Change was coming and no one calmed him, no one told him don't be afraid. Despite being surrounded, he was very alone."

I deliberately quoted Sam Cooke trusting that Jenkins and Grantham had it right.

Mum glanced over my shoulders. "What about the shepherds?"

I gave her a look that expressed my frustration with her.

"Religion is communal as well as individual. He doesn't have a problem with faith per se. It is religion and what the corporate body can do in the name of religion that it would never do as separate individuals. Your dad and I came across a German Pastor called Bonhoeffer in our different disciplines, who explored this with reference to the Nazi regime that imprisoned him."

I stared at the screen again. Shepherds. Shepherds. I frowned, smiled and then continued to type.

"The group sat outside, braving the night's cold, they were always on the outside. Without them society would struggle for they did the menial tasks. But suddenly out of nowhere a divine message of good news. Fear seized them, and at that moment the angel said do not be afraid. Life changing events are to occur, but don't be afraid. Life will never be the same again. You can't control the future, let the changes occur, don't resist them you are part of them. You will witness how new life will live. Do not be afraid. They were treated as equals, respected to be given this one-off message, entrusted with it. They witnessed and shared a moment that was life changing. And yet when the moment ended, they would return to the outside. Unchanged and yet changed. For on the outside it may look like all is the same, the deep underlying changes of life changing. All because they were not to be afraid. Fear would never have taken them to see the changes of life before them. The message to all- do not be afraid. Life is reborn each and every moment. Do not be afraid, for in every new child that is born, life is given a new chance." Send.

The silence was deafening. I had a headache. I rubbed my temples reminiscent of my dad. Before I realised Mum had placed Zapain into my hand. I looked aghast. Paracetamol would have done. She pressed them firmly. She was being Mother and I trusted her. Ping.

"Lovely. Is that what defines Christianity or humanity. What is Christianity's unique festival?"

"Easter." Send. Ping.

"Precisely; resurrection. It is part of the faith. It gives hope for a future that will be better taking away the responsibility of changing the present for the better. So would it be better if actually the resurrection hadn't happened?"

I waited, I paused. There was some logic, but faith isn't about logic. I looked at the Goldfinch on the screen for some kind of guidance.

The security camera was pointed directly at the Goldfinch. I let my eyes focus and it exploded there and then. Ping.

"Sorry. Better off no resurrection. I feel bad." Ping. *"Reconciliation?"*

Chapter Eleven- Reconciliation

I was shattered. I simply typed,

"Coventry Cathedral."

Send. Ping.

"Go on." Came the immediate reply.

"Reconciliation and atonement are different. Your games, your mission seems to be about atonement as a means to reconciliation. It doesn't need to be that way, that is just one view on atonement, very Old Testament. Jesus wanted his disciples, one assumes we are all disciples, to be in union with God, that is reconciled. There isn't good works or righteousness. We can't earn the Kingdom of Heaven. It is given freely so how do we respond? Our response needs to be practical, logical, heartfelt and genuine. Something like this:

Where there is death we must work for life.

Where there is war we must work for peace.

Where there is oppression we must work for liberation.

Where there is hate we must work for love.

Where there is resentment we must work for forgiveness.

Where there is anger we must work for reconciliation.

Where there is stress we must work for calm.

Where there is fear we must work for hope.

Where there is poverty we must work for equality.

Where there is conflict we must work for a resolution.

Where there is pain we must work for healing.

Where there is frustration we must work for empathy.

Where there is intolerance we must work for understanding.

Where there is anxiety we must work for answers.

Where there is propaganda we must demand the truth.
When we are entrenched we must push for development.
Where there is change we must ensure stability.
Where there is violence we must ensure tranquility.
Where there is ignorance we must listen.
Where there is antagonism we must build on commonality.
Where there is diversity we must celebrate the difference.
Where there is conformity we need to look beyond.
When we are exclusive we must open up.
When we think we can't do anything then we must keep going.

In many Shamanic societies when someone goes to the medicine man complaining of being disheartened or depressed he asks, 'When did you stop singing? When did you stop dancing? When did you stop being enchanted by stories? When did you stop finding comfort in the sweet territory of silence?' It is in these experiences we find God. Western society and the religious within it forget all this and this is what you are lamenting with your crusade to change us. To change us, I agree it needs to change, we cannot be pushed, we need to be led. We cannot be cajoled, we need to be cherished. We far too often think we find God in doing good works. We think we find God in being self righteous, in piety."

Send.

I sat back to take a slurp of coffee thinking his response would be a while. It was too quick, perhaps the essence of it had already been prepared, perhaps we were on the same wavelength. Perhaps as Moo had suggested he wanted me to win. Win? What is winning? Ping.

"So let us look where we find Jesus:- at parties, in conversations with the outcast, liberating sinners in the dark quiet places where we don't want to look. In the pain, the isolation, the unwanted. In the unjust times, the unfair times

this is where we find God. And in those unwanted dark and quiet places we stop, we slow down, we adjust our eyes and wait in stillnesses til we see clearly. It is in the stillnesses we recognise God in other places. And what is God? God is love of everything, every-time, everywhere."

I understood so responded.

"So to be in union with God is to recognise God in the places we don't want to look and bring God's love to those places. That is to be in union, in union with God, in union with love, truly reconciled, a life reconciliation that transforms us." Send. Ping.

"Touché." Ping.

"Don't worry about any explosion, I couldn't do it, not there, not that place so there isn't one. Go home, all of you. Drink a glass of wine; white for you I'm guessing."

"Rioja, red." Send. Ping.

"Enjoy. Have a good night."

I walked into my own flat which I hadn't seen for days. It should have been dark but was illuminated by candlelight and the aroma of a chilli cooking. No one else had a key but I did keep one under a plant pot outside. I didn't bother to check if it was there, there was little point.

"Hello?" I called.

"Kitchen," came the recognisable voice.

I didn't go to the kitchen. I walked to the small second bedroom I had set up as an office. My computer was on and a laptop that wasn't mine synchronised together. When my sisters started jumping all over the world I made sure with Snapchat that I knew where they were at any one time. Not because of any worries, more that they could all just turn up at your doorstep and expect a home cooked meal, bottle of wine or inevitably a combination of the two. Baydar had all the icons of the phones' whereabouts on the screen including mine. I knew it was him, he was audacious and it explained each time I had an email when we were on the move. As I glanced at the screen I noted with surprise that Sapphire, Filippa and Ruby were all in London, south of the river in a Premier Inn close to the Millennium Bridge. Why were they here? Mum had probably called them but why? I scanned the screen looking for her icon and found it in Guy's hospital. I guess she had friends there.

I was brought back to the moment by the familiar voice. "Your wine is here."

"Won't you join me?" I asked on entering the kitchen.

"I may not be practising but I was brought up a Muslim, some things never leave you." He smiled. "Would you mind getting the soured cream out of the fridge?" He motioned to the fridge as if I didn't know where it was. He had a point. Normally it would have had a bit of mouldy cheese, a Babybel, a bottle of Prosecco and curdling milk. As I opened it I was taken aback. It had been cleaned and was full of food. He noted my face.

"You need to look after yourself."

"Thank you," I murmured.

We sat down to the chilli. I was ravenous. I hadn't really eaten a proper meal for days, possibly months if you ignore takeaways. We ate in silence.

"Tomorrow?" I asked as I pushed the plate away.

He laughed. "Who knows?" And then more seriously, "Probably."

"Thank you for the food. I suppose….."

"No. I don't. It has gone too far. I am a caricature of myself, not that I know who I am. I know I'm not Baydar. That doesn't matter. I am whom I

165

have become."

"I want to know when did you know, when did you realise you weren't Baydar?" It was the obvious question but one that I knew perhaps I would never really have an answer for and one that perhaps I actually didn't need the answer.

He paused. "Before I left Turkey."

"That's what Mum said," I interjected.

His face acknowledged the statement but he continued. "It doesn't matter, I can't remember enough of who I was. Now I can be a cause for change, this invented persona I have adopted. It is all I know and it haunts me. It is me. I want you to always remember, little one, from the aridity of the driest of souls grows a fruit tree in the most extreme of conditions. It is only in this love, the pure love. The self that you truly give and so receive one to another is love. Know that this love is inside you, find the key to unlock it, share it with interpersonal vulnerability and the merging of the souls of love, the merging of sea and sky, river and sea where there is no end; as life nears death it knows that it was. In this moment all feels changed but nothing is, it is the inexorable movement towards a moment that already was, will be, has been; a moment called life."

I broke the silence. "Isn't life itself just a series of questions? Where does it come from? Why are we here? Who am I? When did it? Will it? Has it? You say love is the answer but if love, what? Where? Why? Who? When?"

His thoughts were scanning tangibly across his forehead as he spoke. "Love manifests itself at the moment where the sky meets the sea, where the fruit tree grows in the arid landscape where the unclimbed mountain tops seem reachable and the clouds paint stories across the sky."

I wanted to protect him, to change the course of events that I had foreseen unfolding over the past days. I thought I saw a chink in his armour of emotional logic.

"Yet love needs to be open for it is the catalyst to change and development. Love has a hope that remains undaunted, all encompassing, enveloping and protecting."

His response again maintained the metaphorical stance he was enjoying.

"It is a breeze in a summer's heat, a sheet in a Mediterranean clime. A paradise in a slum of dejection, a strength in a hopeless world." He paused.

I took a tangential stance, "You cannot be given love rather you have to receive it from within, allow it to touch you, change you, not that you become someone else. Au contraire with love you become who you truly are and loved for it."

He saddened. "You are right. perhaps though for some it becomes too late."

Frightened I retaliated, "It is never too late." He brushed the hair away from my face which reminded me of my childhood.

"Do you know the story of the chicken and the eagle?"

He raised an eyebrow.

"Okay, to paraphrase, there is this eagle egg that falls into a nest of chicken eggs. They all hatch some days later and the eagle is raised as a chicken, behaving as chickens do. An ornithologist came across the eagle that thought it was a chicken and encouraged it to break free from its self-imposed shackles and fly. It took a long time but eventually with the scent of freedom, a purpose of a future, one day he stretched out his wings and soared never to return to the barnyard. He truly was an eagle even though he lived the life of a chicken. Just like this eagle people who have learned to think of themselves as something they are not can re-decide in favour of what they really are."

"For me it is too late." He said softly. "The flower will blossom but will always wither and die and give way for one of its buds to blossom. Mauriac wrote in the mouthpiece of Madame Desqueyroux, 'The uselessness of my life: the emptiness of my life: unending loneliness: no way out.' He paused and took my hand. There was no reaction from me. I let it happen. It was as natural as anything had been in the last few days. He looked directly at me.

"But what about the Beatles?"

"What about them?" he inquired.

"Revolution. The Beatles is how I found you.; remember the lyrics? Change the world yes, destruction not fine with me. I started to sing the song gently but tailed off almost as soon as I had started. I had made my point and was struggling with singing solo, suddenly becoming extremely self conscious.

The smile was ingratiating. I relaxed, therefore, just a little.

"You know Teresa of Avila?"

"Remind me," was my coy response.

"Well she said many things but one of my favourites is this one."

He steadied himself in the chair preparing to find somewhere in his memory cells the particular passage he wanted.

"Christ has no body now on earth but yours, no hands but yours, no feet but yours. Yours are the eyes through which to look out Christ's compassion to the world. Yours are the feet with which he is to go about doing good. Yours are the hands with which he is to bless now."

I smiled. "No arguments with that one. Christ's own mystic version of Harriet Tubman." He threw his head back, closed his eyes and roared with laughter.

"I had never quite made that analogy, but I like it." He gently stretched out his hands in front of him. "The evening draws nigh my little one. The sun has set, the sky descends to let us know it is near the end. It is dark and whimsical hiding its many secrets, increasing as time begins to call. The night air beckons, welcoming, chastening, all encompassing. Taking our joys and swelling them into tomorrow. For the measure of the night is found in the talk of the morning. And if it is forgotten out of sight then the moon and the stars are mourning. For the forgotten hours that we have are precious at the end. So take heed, Cariad. Take this night into the morrow. For each night has at its end the joy of the rising dawn. New awakenings are only found from within the experiences of sight, soul and sound. This night is precious now, let the moment last. Take then this night to the morrow. Treasure it all every moment with all your might. May it bring you and I peace; we need to lighten your load with sleep. From the yoke of your burden may you be freed."

He got up. "Do quickly what you must do." And left.

There is a prayer my dad taught me as a child. He said it summarised the faith and merged it with the religion and it is something I can trot out when I'm not sure of a reality yet recognise something behind the "Cloud of unknowing."

"Risen Lord Jesus, your followers recognised you when you broke bread, in the calling of their names. We are called to see you in the forsaken places, situations and people and to share with them your blessing through weakness. Help us to always recognise you in life that we may bring your healing through love, hope and peace."

While I was with Baydar I felt this, feeling something but not quite being able to identify what. I had to put those feelings aside. Now was the issue; who he is now, not the past which is unimportant. He could be Nelson Mandela himself it didn't matter.

When I got to Thames House besides the Team, Moo and Mum were there. Broughton understood my dilemma. Here was a man who did not know who he was, but felt he should live who he had become and yet it was out of gratitude, nothing more. Duty even? No. More through a lack of an alternative. This was not a terrorist but a functional man who had lost himself and therefore only had his function, that had been programmed in, with which to identify himself. Broughton queried several times, the final sentence that Baydar had said.

"What does it mean?"

It was Moo who answered. "Look, here you have got a guy who is apparently anti-religion and yet is quoting the Bible left right and centre. He is over-compensating, that is why he found himself in this mess. That is why he appeared as if he had some kind of psychological problem because he wasn't being himself, he knew it. He found something in his reading which appealed and yet wasn't supposed to. That is why, Ysella, you have been able to win a couple of rounds against him. You were taking the part that he found most natural, who he truly is, is much more akin to who you are."

"Okay," I kind of said, unsure really.

"But how does that answer what he meant by his passing statement?" Broughton reiterated.

"It doesn't, I was just giving context. It's easy though."

"It is?" The rest of us were in unison.

"Concordance please!"

I googled for one, and typed the phrase in; St John's Gospel, Jesus' last words to Judas. There was silence.

Judas has often taken a bad press. Nikos Kazantsakis didn't quite see it that way. Using St John's Gospel as the pivotal point he portrayed Judas as the only one of the Apostles who understood what needed to be done. He was the real friend, the only one Jesus trusted to do it. Certainly Judas in his reflection "The Last Temptation of Christ" is far removed from the pariah that he has subsequently been identified as.

"We have no choice, for the sake of society we need this scapegoat." I said pointedly, more for my own benefit than anyone else's. "And he is giving permission. There really is no way back for him."

"I would still like to find out who he truly is," Broughton responded.

"Was. Who he truly was." My mother injected. "Whoever he was, he isn't that person now, that man died."

The email sounded and we all unconsciously reached for the phone. Broughton, ever mindful of etiquette, let me pick up my phone despite his impulse. One word:

"Salvation."

Salvation, Christians believe, comes from the covenant earned by Christ on the cross. The punitive sacrifice.

"This is the final one then, after his last supper with Judas." Moo did not mean any ill will in her statement, she was simply making the connections.

"So where is Gethsemane, where is Golgotha? Or is it one place for our man?" An email sounded. By this stage Wilson had bluetoothed my phone to a projector and the screen was the white office wall. Everybody looked at the three words now in front of them.

"Latvia say norm"

"Anagram," Broughton stated without a trace of emotion. "Ideas...... people?"

Wilson had grabbed a notepad and was writing the letters down when Moo grabbed the pen from him. On the office wall she took out the S.A.L.V.A.T.I.O.N. We looked at the remaining letters. A.Y.R.M.

It took Moo only a second, "Salvation Army, where are the Headquarters? Are they in London?" She was directing her questions at Wilson who was already typing.

He turned triumphantly, "101 Queen Victoria Street."

"It isn't finished yet!" Broughton scolded him.

I switched the page to maps and looked.

Moo observed, "Right he will go to St Paul's Cathedral, that will be his Gethsemane, and he will walk down Godliman Street out of sheer bravado in his game."

Wilson looked blank

"God-ly-man. A Godly man?" she exhaled.

"So what are you suggesting?" Broughton inquired.

"Let him do what he has planned. That way we know everyone is safe because he doesn't want to hurt anyone, agreed?" We nodded our assent.

"Clear the road we know where he will come from though. Let him get to the Salvation Army offices and see what he has in mind. It is obviously some kind of suicide. We don't want him to be out of control and for an accident to happen."

"And we don't want maximum publicity either." Broughton was adamant.

"Why?" Mum asked.

"The public love an anti-hero, the individual with the lone voice fighting against the Establishment; an incompetent Establishment at that. We need this to go away as suddenly as it came." Broughton had stepped over the edge, this was personal not professional. I was young but I had learnt by osmosis that when you make/take things personally then your world becomes like a downward spiral from which only a miracle will save you. Professional at all times. Perhaps a little bit more personal reflection from me would have have asked more questions of Baydar, more questions of myself. Professionalism kept you slightly detached. The detached observer can see a broader picture, not necessarily a more accurate one. That way I wasn't bogged down in a wild goose chase through minutiae. Minutiae of course has its place, just not now. The room was filled with silence.

"Shall we?" Wilson motioned for us to move. And I guess actually it was the only option. We always had forced the next email when Baydar had realised we had worked out the clue. We were in the cars in two minutes and making our way along the side of the Thames. Outside of the Headquarters of the Salvation Army were already banks of photographers and media. Wilson walked up to them and inquired what they were doing.

"Dalaman Dan's last stand, apparently," one of them confirmed.

Broughton was unhappy, Wilson unable to comprehend. "Emails?" Broughton questioned me.

"No, and I don't think there will be one either."

We waited. We had eyes looking North and East and West. Not from behind, not looking at the Millennium Bridge so Baydar was on Booth's Street, named after the founder of the Salvation Army, before we knew it. When we saw him we noted a padded jacket that was too big and yet fitted snugly.

"Shit," Broughton murmured.

Snipers were arriving on the roof tops above and they were frantically changing positions. The Press there, their cameras already being overworked. Broughton had one hand to his earpiece fifty yards away and I heard his voice in mine.

"Your thinking?" he said.

The final words in my own flat came back to me and I spoke into my headset, "One shot; Take him."

Baydar established eye contact with me, gave a glimpse of a smile in acknowledgment and pressed a button on his phone. The bullet hit at once. The body just rolled to the paving slabs, blood seeping from somewhere. I turned away. The Press were in their element, ghoulish reporters of bad news clicking away frantically. I suddenly felt cold. The body lay there.

Broughton was already striding over to the Press flanked by Wilson and a nameless body guard. He hadn't prepared a statement, except the one of course he had been preparing in his mind since the first bombings. As he composed himself there was a loud explosion and all of the south windows of the Salvation Army Offices shattered and splintered showering the Press amongst others in fragments of glass. Broughton ducked raising his elbows above his head as he did so. An involuntary action that was caught on camera, a picture that would make the front pages of the international press. That and the story of the missing body. Because in the ensuing melee Baydar's body disappeared. All that was left was blood. The Sally Army motto: 'Blood and Fire. With Heart to God and Hand to Man.' Somehow this is what Baydar believed would happen. Why? Did he really believe in what he was doing, or did he come to some other realisation? I will remember his look, that last look, a tender moment that stirred longing in me. I broke down, the grief of losing my dad little over a year before took hold and I wept. I don't know what was happening around me at that time, it was a blur. History was to recall that Broughton looked like a fool, a condition from which he would never really recover.

For now he just sat on the pavement broken, recognising the future that lay before him, "He thought he was going to change the world," he said. "This deception of a missing body will give cause to a greater deception than the first."

I was in a state. It was Ruby who had her arm around me. Where was Mum? Where was Moo? Wilson? I hadn't heard the email come through on my phone. Ruby, by second nature rather than curiosity, checked it. She passed the phone and I stared through the words.

"I'm so proud of you. D"

Epilogue- Reciprocity

Life is a series of reciprocal relationships. If the reciprocity is not equal than there is a disturbance. Disturbances disable as they affect an inner equilibrium. A reciprocal relationship is not held at arm's length, rather you are submerged within it. It becomes your life as it is as natural as breathing. In this relationship the giving and receiving are as natural as the ebb and flow of the tide. That is why relationships where one person is stronger in some fields than the other and vice versa are healthy relationships because together they grow. Western society doesn't encourage reciprocal relationships rather it encourages and rewards the success of the individual. Teams rarely get awarded a team bonus, but individuals within that team do. Reciprocity does not know it is giving, there isn't an expectation of reward nor is there the dreaded guilt as a reason. In fact you don't know you have given. On the other hand we are also bad at receiving and feel we need to give back to pay off the indwelling guilt. Life is full of this relationship. We prune a rose bush for our own ends and in return it flourishes once more. The natural order that ensures that plants and humans so need each other, each other's waste products keeping alive the other. Without this reciprocity we are alone and the loneliness is the pain of the soul. You can be lonely in the most crowded of rooms. Lonely in a stable of activity. Lonely if there is no reciprocity. You may be given to, paternalistically, but without reciprocity in the relationship, it is meaningless. Loneliness accompanies the dark night of the soul and spirals the descent into self oblivion. Identity then becomes so important. Who are we? Once we answer that question in life all other questions take their place. The problem is that in life most of us find it hard to answer once. Answering it twice is unreal though occasionally necessary. No identity means real loneliness, so no reciprocity, therefore no real life. Of course we still exist and that existence can be so hard, desolate, with no direction or understanding of the fullness and beauty of life. Know who you are, or least spend your life trying to refine your knowledge and all other decisions fall into place without you even knowing it. Decisions are the life blood of our existence and very often determine our identity. Let us therefore turn this upside down and reflect a better way; let our identity determine our decisions.

I was blind-copied an email that was issued in Thames House. It was out of courtesy rather than necessity. I appreciated it.

"Charles Broughton has been a faithful servant to the service for thirty years. In the light of recent events he shall be taking a leave of absence. Liam Wilson has been tasked with reporting to the Deputy Director General on the 'Dan Bombings' in liaison with Luke Grantham and Phoenix Jenkins who continue to work with the Turkish authorities. We are grateful for the liaison with Scotland Yard and the deployment of Miss Ysella Mae who has been instrumental in the success of the operations against the terrorist Demir Baydar. She is currently on sabbatical."

Moo received the text whilst she drank a hot Ribena and lemon in the Tate Modern. She texted back, *"Tate Modern cafe."*

Seconds later, Liam Wilson was sat across the table.

"Didn't want to be presumptive," he offered, by way of explanation. She shrugged. It mattered little. "I've been tasked with wrapping this whole thing up, making it look like it all made sense. Especially the last day, especially……..." he tailed off. "I need to tell the truth in a way that protects the innocent, don't I?" He was looking for reassurance. Moo, like her mother, did not play games so gave him none.

"If that is what you must do, of course I will help, if you think I can." A statement.

"Wasn't it good to work together though? You're as sharp as anybody I know. You ought to work for the Service. Maybe I could put in a good word or something?"

"Maybe." She smiled coyly. His rush of enthusiasm reminded her of a little boy who engaged with life in fits and starts.

The report, which took months to write, was full of intricate detail and fact. It took so long that it was old news by the time it hit the desk of the new Home Secretary. It was so deliberately dull that he never got past the fifth page. It had had its desired affect.

On the second anniversary of Dad's last night in Turkey Mum returned from France for a brief trip to St. Colan. She arrived twenty minutes early and had already planted a bay tree on the north eastern corner. It was just her and I. Me in my pink Doc. Martens and Mum in wellies and a wax jacket specifically bought for the occasion. That morning she had walked through the woods treasuring each moment whilst I had been enjoying a glass of water in Trethurgy. The simple pleasures that life is made of. We stood there in the Churchyard, half overgrown allowing nature to flourish. She took my hand. "This is where Dad is," she said, giving it a little squeeze. "Dad is here."